After training as an art a   Brisbane, Annette Lower, a: the charismatic art dealer Ra.......During that passionate affair with Contemporary Australian art and artists, Ray moved the gallery to Sydney in 1984, just at the time Annette became pregnant with their son.

When the marriage failed in 1996, Annette learned the nuts and bolts of book publishing with independent publisher John Kerr, and then became first a theatrical agent, then a literary agent, mentored by the esteemed Rose Creswell. Another passionate affair developed, this time with some of Australia's finest authors. She somehow managed to study part-time at the University of New England for an honours degree in arts between long lunches and reading the slush pile.

In 2004, Annette decided to leave the publishing industry and move to the Sunshine Coast hinterland to farm trees (karma), and is currently on first-name basis with ten chickens, twenty cows, seven guinea fowl and one poet — her partner and creative collaborator, Geoffrey Datson.

Art Life Chooks

LEARNING TO LEAVE THE CITY
AND LOVE THE COUNTRY

ANNETTE HUGHES

FOURTH ESTATE • *London, New York, Sydney* and *Auckland*

Fourth Estate
An imprint of HarperCollins*Publishers*

First published in Australia in 2008
by HarperCollins*Publishers* Australia Pty Limited
ABN 36 009 913 517
www.harpercollins.com.au

HarperCollins*Publishers*
25 Ryde Road, Pymble, Sydney, NSW 2073, Australia
31 View Road, Glenfield, Auckland 10, New Zealand
1–A, Hamilton House, Connaught Place, New Delhi – 110 001, India
77–85 Fulham Palace Road, London, W6 8JB, United Kingdom
2 Bloor Street East, 20th floor, Toronto, Ontario M4W 1A8, Canada
10 East 53rd Street, New York NY 10022, USA

National Library of Australia Cataloguing-in-Publication data:

Hughes, Annette, 1960–
    Art life chooks: learning to leave the city and love the
    country / author, Annette Hughes.
    Pymble, NSW: HarperCollins Publishers, 2008.
    ISBN 978 0 7322 8689 7 (pbk.)
    Hughes, Annette, 1960–
    Country life – Queensland – Noosa Region.
920.72

Excerpt from *Letters to a Young Poet* by Rainer Maria Rilke, translated by
Stephen Mitchell, copyright © 1984 by Stephen Mitchell. Used by permission
of Random House, Inc.
Printed and bound in Australia by Griffin Press
70gsm Bulky Book Ivory used by HarperCollins*Publishers* is a natural, recyclable
product made from wood grown in sustainable forests. The manufacturing processes
conform to the environmental regulations in the country of origin, Finland.

5 4 3 2 1   08 09 10 11

For Rose Creswell

… come close to Nature. Then, as if no one had ever tried before, try to say what you see and feel and love and lose.

… write about what your everyday life offers you; describe your sorrows and desires, the thoughts that pass through your mind and your belief in some kind of beauty …

Rainer Maria Rilke, *Letters to a Young Poet*

Watch out for trucks,
And always work with children and animals
It's more beautiful that way.

Geoffrey Datson, 'Mincemeat'

Contents

Autumn

    1st April   3

    2nd May   29

Winter

    3rd June   57

    4th July   80

    5th August   102

Spring

    6th September   127

    7th October   150

    8th November   171

Summer

    9th December   197

    10th January   217

    11th February   240

Autumn

    12th March   269

Acknowledgments   287

Autumn

1st April

Rainfall last month: six inches

Jobs for this month:

- Sow cool-weather vegetables — 1st: spinach, lettuce, kale, curly endive, dill, celery, broccoli. 6th: cauliflower, snow peas, peas. 18th–20th: turnip, beetroot, carrot.
- Move chooks to front yard.
- Mulch & plant out beds 5 & 6.
- Anniversary dinner! Drive to town & splurge on some good red instead of crappy cask. Get chook food, mulch straw.

It's a big day out in the garden when the chooks move on, but today is bigger because their dome has to move from the back to the front yard. Usually I just drag it and the girls trundle along still inside until the mobile pen is positioned over the next bed in the cycle, usually a move of only about twenty feet, but today is cross-country. So unless I want to spend the rest of the day hunting through the undergrowth catching wayward chickens, Geoffrey and I do it the hard way.

It takes the two of us; he catches the girls in the dome and passes them to me outside, two at a time, from whence they are ferried to a static chook pen in the corner of the garden. When the chooks are all out, we pick the dome up — it's not heavy, just awkward to balance — and carry it out between the side of the house and the water tank, across the driveway, and deposit it on the first bed in the front garden. Then again we go through the ferrying process and, two by two, the birds are carried back to the dome.

They've come to quite like these little adventures, taking in the view and rather enjoying the feeling of flying without all the effort of flapping wings. Or, maybe they're so deeply traumatised they can't move or speak. Who'd know? The eye of a chicken is a difficult thing in which to read an emotional response. I do know, however, that when they are installed in the new position, they are delighted by the fresh food source and cluck excitedly as they forage and scratch around for insects and worms. Their egg yolks turn orange from the greens.

On these spent garden beds grow the remnants of the previous crop — cabbages and broccoli with only the flower heads missing, warragul greens trailing over every spare inch, lettuces bolted to seed, and a range of Chinese vegetables that I plant especially for the girls to graze on. It only takes them a few days to eat everything they want and then flatten it.

The chook dome is an extremely efficient tractor that runs on the broadcast of a handful of seeds. Lots easier than making the ethanol and putting it through a machine to produce the same result. And there are added advantages; the exhaust of my chicken tractor is edible. The eggs are breakfast, and the chook droppings fertilise the next crop.

Once the dome leaves, I plant the bed out and close the fence for three months while the dome does a circuit of the front beds. The fortnightly procession of chook dome from bed to bed has become part of my calendar, marking out my year.

And my reward for today's labour? A shower, washed hair, champagne in the fridge and dinner in the oven. Geoffrey and I are celebrating. I'll put on a dress to remind both of us that I am indeed female, he'll untangle his mop of sun-bleached hair, pull on a good pair of jeans, and we'll start the cocktail hour a little early. We'll watch our flock of free-ranging guinea fowl chatter and graze their way up the slope of the yard to their roost, flap up, one after the other, and argue about who is sleeping where in the spreading poinciana tree. As the light fades we'll listen to the 'twinkle pop of stars' and I'll light the hurricane lamp I keep on the table outside on the verandah. We'll talk and remember that today is the third anniversary of the first day of the rest of our life.

We'd set out from Sydney on the first of April two years ago, our old Valiant Safari chock full of the last of our stuff — tools, bedding, linen and clothes, and at the top of the load, my precious brand-new cello — and headed out of town directly into peak-hour traffic and the soon-to-be-setting sun. April Fools' Day, and we're finally out of there.

With the great Gothic hump of the Harbour Bridge at our backs, I felt an incredible rush of release as we made our escape: rats deserting a ship.

Twenty years of hard labour is as much as any body should have to bear of the relentless round of work, socialising and non-stop hot and cold running sensual and intellectual titillation that is Sydney. It was great when I was young and optimistic and immortal, and egocentrically believed that the universe was spun around a brilliant core, which was me, but I'm not that creature anymore. I came to see the city as a magical, glittering mirage that had seduced me into believing I was completely essential to its existence, while it was really a cruising shark always on the move, sucking the energy of its inhabitants through its gills. When that perception kicked in, I went into self-preservation mode, and as much as I love my girlfriends, and the endless colour and movement of that other life, it felt like the right time to leave. I was already emotionally packed. All that remained was to load up my material baggage and get the hell out of town. As it was, we'd already retreated from the pleasures of city life.

I'd met Geoffrey some three years before we moved in together. I'd divorced and so had he, and as we licked each other's wounds, I found myself falling for this strange, quiet, gentle creature. He's a poet, but I didn't know that at the start. He worked as a set builder during the day to raise enough cash to fund his obsession.

It was only when I lived with him in his warehouse studio and listened to him night after night, working on his recordings, that I began to understand that he was the real thing — an artist. Somehow he was surviving on an average of about four hours' sleep each night. Outside the studio, the warehouse was crowded and noisy during the day. His window of opportunity to work ended as garbage trucks and the first trains into nearby Central Station broke the fragile white silence of the few hours after midnight. You can still hear the sirens and mournful train horns embedded in his music from that time.

I worked all day in the service of writers, as a literary agent, and spent most of my evenings glued to manuscripts. I'd get home late from a book launch or a publishing dinner, and he'd be there, weaving a weft of words into the warp of his electronic loops, shot through with his silken blue guitar. It was the only place I wanted to be, rapt in the sound of his voice and his music. The studio became the still centre of my universe; a snug refuge from the city's stormy intensity. We'd stopped going out, hadn't seen a movie in a year, lived on takeaway food from Chinatown and I drank far too much — my red wine diet: you drink as much red as you like and eat only that which goes with red wine.

Added to that, what my job held in terms of huge professional satisfaction, interest, and deep and loving relationships with my best girlfriends, clients and colleagues, it lacked in financial remuneration. Sydney was getting just too expensive to survive. Something had to give.

When Geoffrey's father rang to say that the house at the bottom of the hill was vacant and ask if he was interested in coming up for a couple of months to do some maintenance work on it, I felt a cool draft of possibility on my face and we decided to rent it ourselves and go for good.

So, here I am, holding a rose and a feather, like the fool in my tarot deck in the midst of life's journey. If I was a

New Age type, I'd revel in the symbolism of it — the rose and feather representing my heart and soul as my only map for the trip. But I'm not. I just look foolish, an April fool, and I'm just holding an ordinary garden-variety rose, the first bloom of the season from the three bushes I've planted, one each year at the entrance to my garden, to remind me of Rose, my much-loved friend and mentor. And the feather is to make an arrow flight for young Christopher down the road.

Here we are in paradise. Not a symbolic one, a real one, in which everything is a riot of green, filled with animals and birds and the odd human. Here we're surrounded by an infinite variety of life forms other than Sydney's cockroaches, pigeons and people. Although we also have a few pests, I'm learning their ways and they pretty much keep out of mine. The only creatures I'm wary of are insects and reptiles, but I try to make sure our paths don't cross, and if they do, we both keep a respectful distance.

There is only one predator higher up the food chain than me and I can't even see it — bacteria. If the power goes down and I don't realise, the food in the fridge gets pongy and has to be chucked out. We keep a saucer with an ice cube on it in the freezer to tell if the temperature gets below melting point.

I don't imagine a dramatic end — I doubt that Budget (our bull) will trample me in a fit of temper, although he easily could. I won't disturb a sleeping king brown and go out in a spasm of snake venom, though it is a possibility. I'm Zen enough to know that it will probably be some microscopic monster that takes me out. Blood poisoning from a barbed-wire scratch or something equally boring will get me in the end. Worst thing that has happened so far is that my back went out from a prolonged bout of violent sneezing, caused by the hay fever I get at certain times of the year. Three days in bed is the only cure. And if I leave the house without a slimy layer of tropical-strength insect repellent, I get covered in itchy mozzie bites which, if not treated carefully, can ulcerate and become infected. Ticks the size of a pinhead are hard to avoid, and it's almost impossible to see them once the head is buried. I come up in enormous swollen welts that take weeks to subside, leaving a hard, itchy little lump under my skin.

I've grown mindful since being here. Death never occurred to me in Sydney, but now I've reached that point in life where elderliness is suddenly a lot closer than youth, I'm appalled by the idea that my time on this planet might be running out. If I was Buddhist, I'd be able to get my head around it and know it's just my ego preventing me from understanding that life and death are only transitional states, but I'm not — I'm just your regular, egomaniacal, carnivorous tree-changer, so I'm working on risk-minimisation.

Hence the introduction of the guinea fowl, or 'Minipecks', as Geoffrey has fondly renamed them. Their main function in life is to patrol the perimeter and keep the ticks down. They are excellent pest controllers, capable of picking grasshoppers off the tallest broccoli plant without actually breaking it or digging up the garden beds. In exchange for their labour they live in this pleasant valley with the tame humans who put food out regularly in the afternoons and find their behaviour deeply amusing.

This time in 2004, Sydney was just in the past and the farm still miles ahead and we were hurtling through a roaring hollow of present tense. I'd been to the farm on holidays, but had only ever driven past the house where all my stuff was now waiting in boxes and bubble wrap. I tried to imagine what it was like under that big square green roof nestled below the dirt road, a curtain of deep green vine-tangled bush its backdrop. As to the interior, all I had to go on was a rough plan drawn up by Geoffrey's mother, so for the first 300 miles I played mental chess, moving furniture around from room to room. With only two dimensions to go on, I had no idea of the high–ceilinged interior, cool depths and sprawling size awaiting us.

At Armidale, though, halfway through the journey, I remembered I was also halfway through my life. Suddenly I felt queasy in the stomach, not car sick, but nauseous from a gnawing discomfort, like an oyster irritated by a grain of sand. I kept trying to dislodge it, wear it down and smooth its edges, but still, I was sick with the question:

What am I doing?

Being a Leo, a cat, I always thought I had plenty of lives up my sleeve. I've lived so many of them and played so many roles: daughter, student activist, musician, wife and mother, divorcee, worker in the art and publishing worlds. Now, embarked on yet another version of myself, it struck me: I only have one life left. On my way to it along a winding highway, my trail blazing behind me, I'd left my friends, my career and my whole idea of self, for what? Some half-baked hippie idyll? I would be living in close proximity to the family I'd barely seen since leaving home some thirty years ago, not to mention having Geoffrey's family at very close quarters.

What was I thinking?

I kept my panic to myself while we just kept driving, swallowed up by our own escape velocity. By the time Geoffrey was tired, all the motels were closed, so I took over the wheel while he slept. An eerie purple-black mist at the top of the range closed in around the tunnel of the headlights, transforming the road into a wormhole, sucking me through space. It took all my concentration to see the way ahead; no room in my mind for doubt, just the driving. Finally, past Glen Innes, I couldn't stay awake any longer, and pulled off the highway. It was freezing as I curled into the sleeping-bagged bulk of Geoffrey beside me on the bench seat.

At first light he was up, taking a piss. Through the ice on the windscreen, I could see him silhouetted against a pale watercolour-washed dawn. He took the wheel, I shuffled to the passenger side to sleep again.

By Stanthorpe, I woke up — shocked by my first thought: How will I live with the isolation of this move? What am I going to do without the buzz of a book launch, and being the first person in the whole world to read a new novel? How will I exist without the company of brilliant minds, and the intimacy of friendship, and mad drinking nights out in the Cross with the girls, where we'd talk shop, have ideas and share confidences?

What have I done?

At the bottom of Cunninghams Gap, we pulled over to stretch our legs in a park just outside Ipswich. The morning was mild. My fingers thawed around a mug of coffee from the thermos and, in the trees above us, magpies sang a Go Betweens melody, a magical acknowledgment of our arrival at the outer regions of homeland.

In the stop-start rhythm of Brisbane traffic, I remembered a big reason for leaving — the city itself — and as we made our way through the familiar suburbs of my youth, I remembered why I left this particular city once, too. It was for the sake of art. But this time, it would be the pursuit of my own, not other people's. Mine and Geoffrey's. We'd discussed it endlessly and convinced ourselves that we could imagine something bigger, or realer, or at least just less harrowing than subsisting in Sydney.

By Nambour, the gentle climb up into the rolling hills of the Sunshine Coast hinterland lured me back into childhood. The change of landscape from stark, mean, Brisbane valley flats to the inviting green of the foothills of the range beckoned recollection. This was a holiday place. Every year, rain, hail or shine, each school holiday and every possible weekend in between, my family drove this stretch of road to camp by the Noosa River. Brisbane was where we worked and slept — the river was where we lived. It was where our fondest familial moments converged, deep in the physical world of the river and its shores — immersed in the elements all day, finding shells, flowers and stink bugs, fishing, and spending plenty of time playing with the grown-ups. I thought about the bright opportunity of reconnection with my sisters, who'd also moved up here, and I felt like I was heading home.

I opened the house plan on my lap, but it only took a few moments for my retina to reverse out from the bright morning glare reflecting off the page. In the momentary darkness behind my eyes, the plan's negative image lingered for a moment, then snapped into three dimensions. At least I knew the house was real.

It was moved from Cooran, a town about ten miles north of here. I'd seen fading photo album snaps of the old Queenslander split like a melon down the middle, its halves arriving on two flat-back semis. We can still see the join in the floor, and marvel at how difficult it must have been to match it all together, chock it up on jacks and stump it, re-roof and re-clad. Geoffrey's dad, Joe, rebuilt it all by hand, day after day, and in the process has locked up the carbon in its materials for at least another fifty years.

He placed it perfectly on the block, with the house facing north and straddling a steep hill. One side is only a step up from the ground, and the other side, high up on stumps with enough space underneath to park the Valiant out of the weather.

It has a deep-eaved verandah, lots of rooms and a chimney, but until we arrived, it was still a bit of a mystery. Now its walls are hung with pictures and my big pine table groans under the weight of books, flowers, seed box and diaries. We sleep in the front room, which spans the width of the house. I can't imagine sleeping in a small, darkened room when there is sunrise to wake to.

Opposite our bed hangs one special painting. In a pink moonlit dusk, two figures illuminated by the glow of a hurricane lamp are in the midst of a hilly landscape. A bulbous-bellied creek snakes through a tree-lined gully and empties into a dam. The figures are out looking for something, and a possum in a tree has caught the attention of the woman. Below its branch, a cow wades knee-deep in the dam, and another, only its reflection visible in the painting, stands on the shore just out of frame.

It is a modest picture, small and intimate. It is by the painter William Robinson, famed for his strange fish-eye lens view of the landscape. But he is right: when you are in it, out in the valley, trees really *do* corkscrew up out of hillsides, and from below, their trunks do stretch up and away from you and foreshorten into the sky. The sky really is contained by the enclosure of rising hills, and the dams really do reflect it all; a world within a world, a mirage, a trick of light.

When I saw it in the exhibition, I kept being drawn back to it. There were larger, more impressive and important works in the show, but this one, with its limited palette of muted pinks and mauves, burnt sienna and cobalt shades, holds in its stillness an image of mystery and wonder. The attitude of Bill and his wife, Shirley, out in their landscape in the fading light, intrigued me and resonated with emotional feeling and a spiritual devotion to place.

There is something sacred and metaphysical about it, like a prayer or a chant embodied in the myriad tiny brushstrokes of colour, all laid down with equal intensity to form a dense matrix for reflection. I sometimes lie in bed and watch it change its blush as the sun rises, imperceptibly at first, and then pours into the room. The picture comes to life, shadows form, contrasts heighten and it appears to move. It is a rare privilege to have such a thing in one's life, a work of art that is never static, which reconfigures to serve my own imagination, and accretes meaning the longer I look into it.

When I first saw it, I had no idea I would end up living it. Now the female figure is *me* pointing, looking out into the landscape, and Geoffrey holds the lantern as we become illuminati of our place. Once the plantation was just a forest, the valley just a feature of the terrain and the cattle dotting the fields merely decorated the pastoral scene. But now I know it like a lover. I've counted the trees and noted which need to be culled. I know the lemon scent of *citriodora* as I pass beneath the stand. I know the sharp shoulder of the track on the southwestern ridge that leads precariously down to the western paddocks, where lantana grows big as a house. I know where the storms come from and the way they circle the valley, and the shock of freezing rain on hot skin. And it feels like home.

The first project I resolved to undertake was to plant a garden. Not one of those decorative jobs with beautiful useless flowers, but a garden of food plants. I'd never had the time or the space for such a thing before. My Sydney terrace garden was paved, save for a row of narrow raised beds that formed a decorative edge to the pocket-handkerchief backyard. It was fertile enough because the sewage backed up with monotonous regularity, filling the yard with sludge. A few persistent plants managed to cling to life without much help from me. It even once housed a couple of chickens I'd bought at Paddy's Market for my son's amusement when he lived with me there. They pottered about in it and were fond of watching television through the glass doors at the back, but he lost interest when they stopped being cute. Though ostensibly a city girl, I had prior experience of culling chickens, and had no qualms about turning these into a Thai curry, which he resolutely refused to eat.

Linda Woodrow's *The Permaculture Home Garden* is my bible now. I'm a bit of a school project queen, and being a great believer in the book, with all the instructions set out in black and white, I figured all I had to do was follow her directions like a recipe and *voilà* — instant gratification. *Yeah, right.*

It has taken two whole years just to get the hang of it, to condition the sticky clay soil, carve out its form, establish fruit trees. To figure out how to manage the rotations so nothing is planted in the same patch of ground as last year, and build my physical strength up to a point where I can actually go out and do the hours of sweat-drenching slog it takes to maintain it. It makes the potatoes and onions down at the supermarket look pretty competitively priced, but the point is to eat real food. I've pumped so much poison through my body in the past thirty years, it's time I started thinking about repairing the damage that has started to show. If I want to continue with the red wine diet, I'd better start attending to the food side of the equation.

Philosophically, permaculture is about sustainable organic gardening — no pesticides or fertilisers, and building up humus-rich soil by the constant addition of organic matter. Even weeds become valuable in this system. There's lots more to it, but the idea of not actually spending any money on the project is what does it for me.

I didn't find the 'bible' till halfway through the first growing season. My initial attempt was your conventional everything-in-neat-traditional-rows idea of a vegetable patch, all order and regimentation. Geoffrey rented a cultivator and spent a day turning over the densely packed earth of the backyard, and I mounded it into rows with a shovel and half an idea. I couldn't believe it when, right on cue three months later, I was pulling carrots, snapping off broccoli and picking fistsful of snow peas, sugar snaps and silverbeet.

There was an existing chook yard beside the site selected for the garden, which I populated with the 'Coven' just as soon as Geoffrey finished building their accommodation. It's a beautiful safety-orange house with laying boxes we can access from the back by lifting a flap, with an impressive verandah awning at the front. But they don't live there anymore, and I feel dreadful about having moved them into the 'chicken tractor' required by the new system. Geoffrey went to so much trouble building their orange house.

The Coven is named for the drinking club of girlfriends I left behind in Sydney: hens Jane, Linda,

Burridge, Ali, Rachael and Barnsey. These chooks were always part of the uber-plan I'd formulated before leaving.

When I was an art student, one of my lecturers had a standard trick he no doubt used every year to suck his students in. He was a medieval and renaissance nut, and one day, as we were all filing in to our desks, he proceeded without a word to crack an egg into a bowl, separate the white and roll the yolk from one open palm to the other. By this time he had everyone spellbound. Still silent, he then pinched the yolk's membrane between thumb and forefinger, suspended it above another bowl, and with a scalpel split the skin and let the creamy yellow yolk dribble onto the clean white porcelain. Only then did he begin his lecture on tempera painting.

I've been fascinated by that technique ever since. I love the strange, greasy, enamel-like surface that egg tempera produces on a chalky gesso ground. But you can only rely on very fresh eggs for the strongest binding elements. I'd decided that when I got here, I was going to devote some time and energy to mastering that forgotten technique. I would take a year off from working in the outside world and apply myself to seeing if I could do it. I had loaded myself up with jars of pure pigments, beautiful as jewels — and now the Coven's job was to provide the eggs.

During that first year, all my plans of resuming my long-lost ambition to be a painter amounted to precisely nothing. I'd funded myself for a year out of the world, and that doesn't come cheap. It's a big investment to make to achieve no result. Soon a great big monkey of guilt started following me around, accusing me of copping out and being filled with sloth; a failure, a procrastinator. It drives me crazy that Geoffrey can spend hours down in his studio obsessively hooked into his music making, while I'm upstairs making lists of things to do in an effort to avoid having to confront what I'd convinced myself I came here for. I did force myself into my studio for a while, working on the theory that if nothing is going on, do anything, just don't leave.

I finished one painting in oils I'd started in Sydney, prepped and gessoed many boards, fiddled, doodled and took great delight in the process, but managed not to imagine one single image I thought worth the effort. Besides, it cut too much into this new growing obsession — my garden. I'd find myself constantly staring out at it from my studio window, imagining it into existence, planning, thinking, scribbling designs for it onto my sketchpad. I suppose I could have painted that, but I was too preoccupied with the reality of making the garden happen, and it still fills up my whole windscreen, as well as rearview and side mirrors.

We farm trees, sylviculture; such a poetic word, with its romantic association of nymph-inhabited groves. It's one of the reasons behind Geoffrey's decision to return to the family farm. The plantation is among the first Landcare farm forestry projects in the area. The initial crop went in about ten years ago, a second hillside of trees is three years old. During our last visit before moving, Geoffrey had realised that, following a heart bypass, Joe was finding the physical labour of farming a challenge. Back in Sydney the struggle to continue to survive on too little money was fruitless anyway, and Geoffrey felt it was time to help out. It was the house becoming available that sealed the deal.

From the kitchen I watch him sitting high on the old tractor, loaded up with coils of fencing wire, chainsaw, scythe and hoe, heading up into his cathedral of trees to prune their lower branches so they'll grow with minimal knots in the wood. I was secretly afraid we might get bored with this country life, every day the same chores, the same faces, the lack of diversion, but he seems to thrive on it. I see him disappear beneath the canopy and hear the engine stop. He'll dismount, work across a couple of rows, and then fire it up again and move further up the hill. The gradient is so steep it's dangerous to drive across the rows, especially in wet weather, but he's got a handle on the safety issues now, so I'm not anxious about it anymore.

I have never seen Geoffrey more delighted than when he returns from a morning tending the trees. His conversation often includes an amusing story about the antics of the young heifers that are pastured in the tree paddock to keep the grass trees grazed down. For most of his working life he has been a builder, chopping up wood to make sets that are junked the moment they are captured on film. To now find himself growing timber is slowly repairing the damage that so much enforced waste had done to his soul.

He was a teenager when the farm was purchased, and he had helped clear it of groundsel and lantana, living alone out in a shed for a couple of years doing the hippie thing, till his parents moved up permanently. He left to find his fortune, as young men do, while for the next twenty-five years his parents slashed, planted, raised cattle and transformed the wreck of a degraded landscape into the beautiful Eden it is now. It has been lovingly tended, every inch of it walked over and regarded. Their frugal husbandry is evident in the handmade ingenuity of fences and sheds. Stacks of timber are neatly piled beneath sheets of salvaged corrugated iron, and every conceivably useful piece of hardware is saved. Old tools are rebirthed and machinery meticulously maintained in perfect working order. Nothing is ever thrown away until it is completely clapped out. And there's a diabolical stash of aged mango pickles under the house that could be legal tender, it's so good.

One Christmas before moving here, we camped up on the top paddock instead of staying with his parents. We had a mad scheme to rebuild an old shed that had fallen down, and use it as a place to stay for holidays instead of clogging up the family home that invariably filled with Geoffrey's two younger sisters and then-baby nephew. The shed had been built by a previous owner, a bean farmer who lived there for a time. It was small, but had a tank and an orange tree had grown up behind it. The site is just far enough back from the edge of the ridge so that the wind, which blasts up over the steep range from the plain, doesn't touch down again till it hits the hill above. Three big hoop pines crown the crest of the eastern ridge and, below, the vista undulates down to the sea, framed by two mountains, the eroded plugs of a spine of old volcanoes that continue north from the Glasshouse Mountains.

In the sultry late afternoon we'd walk to the top of the western ridge and sit and watch the cattle grazing in the horseshoe valley below. My eye followed gullies down through dappled shade along cow paths as we listened to birds practising their calls. It drives them nuts if you mimic them, throwing your own variation into the mix. They stop, pause, then start the cycle over again, each trilling voice coming from a different part of the bowl of space in their established pattern. I have no idea what they look like, or what their common name is. We call them the Orchestra birds. Likewise the elusive Reversing bird, which sounds like the insistently present beep of a garbage truck. There are invisible Audience frogs in the dam which mimic the sound of one hand clapping, but when it rains and they all go for it at once, they sound like the report of applause sharpened by its passage across the surface of the water. All this is underpinned by the omnipresent shrill, silvery singing of cicadas and crickets, and the low honey-hum of a million bees in the flowering trees that grow near the cattle yards.

From the top of this ridge we'd wait for the evening sky to refract every colour of the spectrum of light fading to violet, anticipating the moon's rise above the earth's own inky shadow on its atmosphere. Back then, I never dreamed I'd be living in the midst of this daily parade of breathtaking spectacle, or that I would come to want to feel its pulse and know its voice.

It was a magical setting for a summer of love that grew deeper as we slept under an ancient green canvas tent, or the stars.

Back in Sydney, a song emerged from the studio:

Long before the sun
the children are asleep, we are the reckless ones.
Out in the field with birds,
under pine trees, what are we hoping for?

The map we've got is wrong,
people just aren't like that anymore.
There's a lot of loose ends
but you can bet that all this has been before.

Let me take you home,
the shoes you're in, the earth you're standing on.
What does it mean to them? Not much,
but between you and me it's everything.

I listened to it over and over, aware that it belonged to both of us — the first time I felt I shared in the perception of an other, without realising just how prophetic it was. Now that I am here, home, back in the same skin I wore as a child who knows the feeling of this place, this northern clime, between you and me, it *is* everything.

2nd May

Rainfall last month: a measly half inch

Jobs for this month:

- Sow — 2nd & 3rd: spinach, endive, green & purple sprouting broccoli, celery, parsley, silverbeet, cauliflower, Vertus cabbage. 12th: snow peas, Telephone peas, dill. 17th & 18th: chives, beetroot, turnips, leeks.
- Pot up sprouted seedlings.
- Move sprinklers to new beds.
- Move chooks along to bed 3 front garden, & plant out with cool weather crops.
- Push the young heifers into the mango paddock.
- Clean out fireplace & start woodpile.
- Take the Minipeck house down.
- Collect seaweed down at Noosa to make foliar spray.

Autumn approaches at last, two months late. But, ah, the welcome relief of it, the sudden change and its promise of winter crops. Early morning is crisp and cool till the sun comes up, and the evenings are perceptibly shorter.

My seedlings don't get singed, and I get to wear my Uggies in the evening — formal footwear up here, practically a fashion statement, which, like thongs, go with everything. Not long now till the deliciousness of a fire at night.

I wonder how the Minipecks will fare in the winter. They are roosting up high in their tree at night now, so it should be safe to dismantle their shanty. They aren't like chickens, which seek shelter and will gladly go inside at night to be locked safely away from predators. The Minis are brave, foolhardy creatures. They prefer to stay out under the stars, and even as youngsters resisted all our efforts to chase them into their box of an evening. So Geoffrey constructed a wildly exotic aviary for them, made of chicken wire stretched over a triangular bamboo frame, with high perches to keep them out of the way of the feral cat.

Eventually, as they grew, one face of the wire was removed so they could free-range in the garden during the day and come back to their enclosure to be fed in the evening and then flap up to their perch at night. Now that they've graduated to the tree above, they require very little maintenance at all. Geoffrey's mother will be pleased — their slum was, I have to admit, a bit of an eyesore.

But that can wait. First job this morning is to push the young heifers through two paddocks and down over the dam wall to the yards. Usually Geoffrey tends to the cows. He patrols the boundary looking for broken fences, opens and shuts gates to rotate them from one paddock to the next and keeps an eye on their movements. But occasionally they need to be herded and I help out. I never miss an opportunity to get up close and personal with the cows. And today is a pretty special occasion — Budget and Number One are to be married.

Budget's number, allotted when he arrived on the farm, is 99. Rather than take the herd numbering system into three figures (which won't fit on their ear tag so it can be read it at a distance), the first of the calves to be born after Budget was numbered one. She is also our first born, the first calf Geoffrey and I came across as a day-old bundle curled up in the long grass, bleary, shaky and brand spanking new.

We are extremely fond of Number One, which has become her name now, leading her to believe that she is the boss; she pretty much considers this her farm. After they were weaned, she and her little band of fellow calves spent much of their first two years in the tree paddock across the lane from our house. Most days I'd visit them with a handful of lucerne or orange skins (which is the calf equivalent of red iceblocks), so they'd learn to come when I call. Soon, Number One allowed me to stroke her neck and ears and could reliably lead her siblings through the gate to the next paddock.

We usually only keep the steers from each year's crop of calves. When they are old enough, the boys join their bigger brothers at the other end of the farm, where they grow into prime rump.

However, because Number One and her seven sisters are off the previous bull and unrelated to Budget, they can join the breeding herd. Till today, the girls have had to be pastured out of sight and earshot of him, but now that they are old enough to flirt with him and suffer the consequences, they get to stay in the pleasant valley with the permanent water and excellent camping spots, and embark upon their new life of relentless motherhood.

Budget is so called because he arrived on the eve of the federal budget two years ago. The following week, while shopping down at the local supermarket, we realised the tragic irony of his naming. There, in the meat section, was a whole shelf of smoothly plastic-film-wrapped trays of meat with big yellow stickers plastered across them:

Budget Beef.

It will be his fate eventually, but for now he gets to spend his days with his nose planted firmly beneath the tail of his choice of nineteen breeders, judging which one is ready for the service only he can provide.

I've known the herd only for this short space of time, but they've rather graciously accepted me into their society, which, if you hang out with cows long enough to observe, is rich and complex. They all have distinct personalities, even though I can distinguish most of them only by the numbers on their ear tags. But I know Panda, with her white face and a black nose and patches round her eyes. She's smart and inquisitive, and often gets the child-minding gig. They have it all worked out. The mothers leave their nippers with the young heifers so they can go off and graze frantically to keep up their milk supply. Occasionally Budget gets the job, but I don't think his heart is in it, although he does seem to display a patient affection for the calves as they skitter about his feet.

And they have the most extraordinarily fine motor control, even the babies. Panda can delicately scratch her nose with the tip of her back cloven toe, and they have this brilliant capacity to get their tongue right up inside their nostrils. What kid wouldn't love to be able to do that and cut out the middle man? Like a big long index finger, they use it to scratch itches, and to caress the calves who stand there, their little tails curled up in ecstasy, as their mothers lick them all over with their big scratchy loofah-like tongues, especially the insides of oversized ears. And it looks like it feels like cow-eyed, mucusy, slobbering love.

Cows gestate for about the same length of time as humans and their babies are just about as adorable as ours. I sometimes visit the snoozing herd in the heat of the afternoon. They come down to the big dam to loll about under trees and chew cud. I have no idea what is in that stuff, but it must be pretty fermented judging by the faraway look in their eyes as they sit, staring vacantly into a middle distance of stoner serenity. While they are off their faces, they don't mind me sitting among them, and ignore the fact that their children's curiosity is getting the better of them. If I sit still, the calves sneak up from behind till they are close enough for me to feel their hot milky breath on my neck. The bolder ones, dewy nostrils quivering, edge even closer and nibble my clothing, trying to taste and smell what this 'not-me' creature could be.

I've been here long enough now to feel comfortable about calling Geoffrey's mother by her first name: Helen — the face that launched a thousand ships. I find this amusing since she not only married a sea captain, but spawned one as well! All her children are keen sailors.

Helen has kept a record of every cow that has passed through the valley, starting with three original heifers and a bull. I am fascinated by their breeding, curious about which traits have been passed on; whether bad habits can be bred out. She has shown it to me a couple of times, and with the excuse of wanting to know which was Number One's mother, I try once again to get my head around the complexity of the system.

She opens the old ledger and running her finger across to Number One's entry tells me her mother was sold soon after we arrived, and reads out how many calves she'd had. She then recounts the names of other cows, like Anni and Versary who had been named on the occasion of a milestone wedding anniversary, and cows that had been named for exotic ports that her eldest daughter Liz had visited when first at sea as a ship's captain. There's a cow called Bakisa for the time her youngest, Joanna, did a diving course, and one called Usa, because in the year of her arrival Geoffrey went to try his luck in New York. But the most romantic is Excalibur, named for her own story of the lady in the lake.

It was late afternoon, the rest of family had gone out, and it had been raining. The banks of the dam were slippery, and Helen could hear a cow bellowing. From the verandah she couldn't see what was wrong, so she walked over to the dam to investigate the racket. As she got closer, she saw the wide, terrified eyes of an extremely distressed cow fixed on her floundering splashing calf. It had slipped from the muddy ledge and couldn't get back up onto the shore. Forgetting that she was alone on the farm, and not really sure of the depth of the dam, she waded into the murky water, to the aid of the bovine mother's drowning baby.

They may look small compared with their mothers but a newborn calf is all dense muscle and much heavier than it seems. So there was no way Helen could push its weight up onto the bank, or pull herself up without letting go of the calf, which was, by now, exhausted and likely simply to sink. All she could do was wedge herself waist deep between two trees on the bank, hold the calf's head above water and wait. And wait. And wait.

Eventually the family returned, surprised to find her not at the house. It took some considerable time for them to settle their own bustle and noise enough to hear both mothers' plaintive calling for help from the dam.

As Helen comes to the end of her tale I realise that she has codified a set of cherished memories in all the names of these cow mothers. The ledger is not just about the cows, not just a tally of numbers and sale prices and dates of births, deaths and sires. Each name is loaded with shared experience, a record of toil and setbacks, joy and love, a time capsule of life on the farm. Her children know its secrets and mysterious connection to their lives and receive it as a prayer ...

> *passed forward*
> *mother to son,*
> *son to daughter,*
> *daughter to child ...*

who is Christopher, Joanna's son, Helen's grandson. He will at some stage be led through the history of the cows and told the stories of their names, and will no doubt attach his own memories to their future generations.

Geoffrey's poem about his mother takes on a whole new layer of meaning for me, now that it is loaded up with the image I have of Helen's careful devotion to her:

> *memories of mother,*
> *laid upon mother,*
> *laid upon mother*
> *back into the earth.*

> *The fragile grid of all our race histories*
> *held tender to heart*
> *and wrapped as heirlooms,*
> *silent under care ...*

By naming Number One and Budget, I am now included in Geoffrey's familial continuum. If only I could work out how to situate myself back into mine, as well. My own mother is losing her memory. What if I have returned too late to find *her* heirloom, the one in which I belong?

The ledger shows the breeding of the last few bulls as pure Droughtmaster stock, which is just as well considering the weather recently. It's supposed to be the tail end of the wet season, but the twelve miserable millimetres of rain last month wasn't even enough to wet the ground under the mulch. Thank God for the pump. I am able to pump water up from the small, shallow dam below the house. It still has water in it — just — and today I get about twenty minutes before it sucks the deepest hole dry. I have to make sure I turn it off before the foot valve clogs up with mud and threatens to burn the motor out. The pump pushes its head of water up a sheer height of about twenty feet, and I am eternally grateful that I don't have to bucket it up. I'm not prepared to risk our drinking water on the garden — that's far too precious to squander since rainfall round these parts has become so mean and average.

I love the water tank. It is a big, cool concrete cistern sunk into the ground, always shaded by the house in the mornings, and the screen of bush that borders the gully of an afternoon. There is a small hole into which Geoffrey occasionally lowers a stick to gauge the water level, but I prefer to peep through it and try to catch the image of my eye floating on the still surface below, and listen to the turquoise echo of its dark enclosed volume. It is comforting and more precious than a vault full of gold, our pure, clean, soft elixir of life. I have become so spoiled by the pleasure of it that I can't stomach town water of any concoction.

I have to admit that when we first arrived here, we did suffer a mild Bali-belly response to the change to tank water. I wasn't too neurotic about it though, considering that in Sydney we lived just down the hill from the Surry Hills reservoir, one source of the infamous *cryptosporidium* bloom that panicked the horses down there a few years back. We drank that for at least a week before the authorities owned up and it didn't kill us, so I figure that the few little bugs who've taken up residence in our tank won't either. It only took a couple of weeks till its flora and ours were snuggled up on speaking terms and now I won't drink anything else — apart from red wine, of course, for medicinal purposes.

In our first year, the wet season barely appeared at all, and we had five desperately dry months in a row and then a leaky input pipe, so any water that did fall bubbled up and drained away without making it into the tank. Geoffrey found the leak and fixed it, but rationed washing loads and showers. It got pretty whiffy round here for a while.

All local conversations began with the weather. The postman actually got out of his car to bring me the mail one morning, curious about our veggie patch and how we were managing to keep it alive. As he passed junk mail over the garden fence, the conversation did not include any mention of the US invasion of Iraq or the growing fear and loathing of terrorism at home — no, it was about the weather. No one out here is the least bit terrorised by imaginary 'muslamic' bombers. Their real fear is whether they'll run out of water before the rain comes. Whether and weather — homonyms. We look up at the sky and wonder, weather?

My seedlings are dying of thirst and the ground beneath the thinning carpet of weeds is as cracked as a Year 5 pinch pot, and I'm starting to hallucinate about being at the beach — but really, I'm only staring wistfully at a postcard stuck on the fridge door. *The Sunbaker*, by Max Dupain, that one of the bronzed shoulders. Even though it's black and white, I just know he has a tan.

A whole mess of national iconography is embodied in that image of sun worship: the fallen warrior; the hedonistic nature lover; the laconic, leisurely larrikin; the loner. The strength coiled in those shoulders pitted against the stark landscape symbolic of triumph in the face of adversity. But *The Sunbaker* does have very cute shoulders, suggesting to me in this day and age that there's probably another reading to add to that list — he's so perfect he's just got to be gay, and if he's not, he's bound to have had sex with a bloke who is. Regardless, he's our hero, our true-blue mate, oblivious of everything except the feel of the sand, and the weight of his authority moulding the land to fit his form, completely indifferent to the sun's radiant knife at his back.

He may be a washed-up corpse, caught in the moment before crabs pick at his flesh and the rising tide comes in and washes his impression away forever. Or maybe he's fallen dead of thirst in an outback sandy-bedded creek, flanked on either side, just out of frame, by a flock of rank, emaciated, flyblown sheep, soon to become breakfast to crows. They're funny things, national icons; their interpretation tends to depend on where you are standing and how far away you are when you look at them.

In the past, I'd look up at the sky and think: *What a pretty colour.* In the city that immense ozone vault means nothing more than: *Cool, don't need an umbrella; nice day to go to Nielsen Park for a bit of a swim with Rose after work.* But here, a clear, cloudless sky means a nightmare of anxious anticipation. I'm luckier than most: lots of locals have to go to the town sporting amenities to shower, wash their clothes in muddy dam swill, or they pay for trucked-in water to replenish their dry tanks. It's pretty unromantic being a child of nature when she turns on you like this.

Dorothea Mackellar might love a sunburnt country, but at the moment I'm not sharing her sentiment. Drought would be fine if it were occasionally accompanied by a bit more flooding rain. All that bronzed-Aussie-battler-pioneer rhetoric is terrific so long as you can still turn your tap on whenever you want.

It hasn't been this bad out here for years, certainly not since the area became recently populated by white middle-class baby-boomer coastal retirees like me. We've been heedlessly flushing our dunnies and watering our decorative lantana borders: *You don't need to water lantana, people! It grows to an impenetrable twenty-foot-high tangle on vapour, as far as I can tell; well, ours does anyway.*

We've moved en masse into fertile river valleys and subdivided hilly farmland. Every acreage holder with an off-the-plan ponderosa, American barn-style shed and ride-on mower, maybe a pony or two for the girls, has sunk a bore to water their 'broad-acre landscaping' (yes, that is what they call it). Now there's less ground water to go round. Down on the coast, practically every McMansion has a pool and a half-dozen ensuites, and they just keep developing more and more of the once-wetlands, sucking the water table dry. There's talk about a population cap in our shire, but what we really need is an opulent-display-of-conspicuous-wealth-and-obscene-waste cap.

Noosa used to be so beautiful. Only the most dedicated campers made it this far for their holidays. It took ages to drive the winding single-laned Bruce Highway north past the Caloundra turn-off where most people called it quits. You had to take the coast road if you didn't know the turn-off at Eumundi or have the skill to negotiate the goat track of a dirt road into Noosa over the range. My dad knew all the back roads from the highway and could get us there when all the creeks were up between Brisbane and our longed-for destination.

The Noosa River was virtually pristine just forty years ago — only a couple of boatsheds on the water, a few shops and weatherboard houses along Gympie Terrace. Hastings Street was just gravel, with a fish-and-chip shop and a camping area called The Woods, which went right down to a rock wall where you could sit and fish and watch the trawlers cross the unpredictable

Noosa Bar. We never went there much — we were just kids and preferred the shifting sandbanks of the river. I had my own tinny, crab pots, fishing lines, two sisters for crew, and we'd disappear for the whole day, adrift in our floating world of seemingly endless salty, sunburnt bliss. Besides, that bar was where I lost my first life, and I've been wary of the surf ever since.

It was to be my big adventure; fishing with my dad 'outside' the mouth of the river in Laguna Bay, and I was delighted to be the eldest and allowed to go. Mum wasn't so sure, but I'd be with my dad and the thought of any force greater than him was completely unimaginable to my twelve-year-old self. Dad had negotiated that treacherous bar a million times — but on this day, as my horrified mother watched from the point through binoculars, she saw our boat leap up the face of a huge wave and the spray burst as it broke over the bow. What she couldn't see was the perspex windscreen split, or the wound from the shard that cut my father's eyebrow deep, just above the socket, or the blood streaking down his shirt. And none of us noticed the bilge fill up with the water that had washed into the boat.

There was no mirror on board, so he had to rely on me to tell him how bad it was, and that maybe we should turn back because there was so much blood, and still I was fearless. Out beyond the breakers, rising up and down on the translucent green swell, Dad decided it would be best to go back in. He turned the bow, and waited for the last of the set that would raise the boat enough above the bar to surf over it, back into the river's channel. We were poised, motionless, then he gunned the engine and we caught the wave.

But something was wrong. As the boat surfed down the face of the wave, it just seemed to stop dead, dug its bow into the trough, and my father sailed over me as the boat suddenly broached and capsized — leaving me bobbing about in the air pocket under its upturned hull, a spaghetti of ski-ropes, fishing reels and crab-pot lines unravelling and tangling all around me. Though only twelve, I knew enough about self-preservation to get the hell out of there. I was wearing a life jacket, and after a couple of goes at trying to duck under the gunwhale, I had to take it off, swim out from under the boat and drag the jacket out after me. Thank goodness I did. Dad wasn't wearing one when he was thrown out of the boat, and we were a good mile offshore.

We tried to hang onto the slippery fibreglass hull, but there was no purchase, and we kept being washed off. The tide was still making, and Dad was pretty sure we'd end up on the beach, so we swam for it. I knew I could swim that far. I used to do that distance easily at swimming training. With the tide pushing me, I was certain I'd make it, especially once I got rid of all the clothing I had on. But, having had a chance to work out what had happened, my head filled with spectres of jellyfish and stingrays and, with Dad bleeding so profusely, sharks. I struck out. I just wanted out of that water.

They found the boat halfway up the Teerwah beach, and salvaged the hull. But I shed my childhood out there. My first life floats forever in my discarded clothes, just beyond the breakers, under the glassy surface of the bay; a mermaid in a dream. Whenever I revisit Munna Point and stand where my mother stood, watching helpless as we tempted fate, the whole drama of my adolescent rite of passage unfolds.

I'm back in that dream now because I'm listening to *Life Matters* on ABC Radio and they're talking about those kinds of places, and everyone who gets on air is remembering *their* holiday spot and how simple the pleasures were; how kids can't have that experience anymore because it's all been built up and filled with video libraries and malls and markets for when the bluebottles blow in and there's nothing to do but shop. Their recollections brim with despair at the loss of their special childhood places and nostalgia for how it used to be, and I'm thinking: *Now you know what it's like to have your sacred sites desecrated, now you know how it feels to lose your connection with your place and be pushed off it by someone with power and money and no regard for your sensibilities. Now you know what* sorry *means.*

I seldom go to my sacred site these days, even though it's only a twenty-minute drive. It makes my teeth hurt to see what has been done to its physical beauty. The rock pools at the national park on the headland are unchanged, and Munna Point still looks out onto a stretch of relatively unspoiled estuary and a mangrove-fringed northern shore, but they are the only two remaining places that have any capacity to tap the springs of my memory.

Geoffrey distributes a local magazine once a month, and occasionally takes me on a 'date' to one or the other of those spots. We lash out on fish and chips and I sift through my midden of memory: the time everyone in the camping area had to huddle in the shower block when a big wind blew in; one of those storms that scour the sand off the beaches, leaving nothing but a bed of compressed coffee rock, and dump a deluge of rain for days, flooding creeks and swelling the Noosa River. Next day the north shore was strewn with huge, empty, pink-lipped shells, which were dredged up by the swell.

Then at night in the tent, showered and clean-pyjama'd, I'd lie in the dark and listen to the whine of mosquitoes that braved the pungent fumes of burning coils. Outside, under a soggy, sagging tarp, dimly backlit by an oil lamp, our elders played cards. One would stand, magically pass through the seated shadows and then bend down to open an esky. I'd wait for the tinkle of ice on glass, *shffft*, a bottle being opened and its contents fizzily gurgled into glasses, straining to hear their muffled voices over thuddering of rain on canvas. Though exhausted and muscle-sore, I fought off sleep to eavesdrop, as they told each other stories: of legendary fish that got away, of shipwrecks. And scary stories: a skull found washed up with the seaweed and shells on the beach at Double Island Point, the ghost of a people that returns to haunt the murderers who had herded them to their deaths there, *once upon a time.*

And my earliest memory: a fishing trip with my parents — my youngest sister, a tiny baby, asleep right up under the bow of the boat, and the other huddled up with me under a tarp — as the rain pelted down into our rented wooden chatter-boat, the floor alive with silver-slapping, gasping bream.

And I remember endless days of snap and Monopoly and buckets under the holes in the tent, and king tides which rose above the grassy shore, and mud crabs and flathead big as dinosaurs. The fish are few now: the mangrove swamps are just about gone, to get rid of sandflies, so the fish breeding grounds are diminished, along with the breeding grounds of memory.

Does the family share it? Do the same images flood their recollections? My lovely little sisters, the small humans who were my colleagues then, are now women with lives utterly different from mine. I can count on one hand the number of occasions we've seen each other since I left home all those years ago. How on earth will we ever get back to scratch with so much water under our bridges? How will we ever negotiate the chasm of time that lies between us, with our sacred site almost gone?

I have watercolour memories of childhood — or perhaps I only remember the ones that are coloured by water? — the relief of rain splashed on the page of monotonous heat and dust, giving it depth, darkening the earth, softening the light and screening the sharp and constant glare. Water, seeping into all my cracks, and along with it, skin-memory of place.

The lake system has become a toilet that needs flushing. It needs to rain for forty days and forty nights to fill up the aquifers. I want to be flood-bound for at least two weeks so it can seep down through the dense clay soil, collect in underground streams and flow into buried caverns. I don't care how many tins of baked beans I have to consume because I can't get to town. Of course, if my wish ever does come true, it's not going to be pretty down on the coast, where suburb after creeping suburb will be sunk beneath swirling brown water; bridges washed away, sewerage plants inundated. Billions of dollars' worth of swank luxury apartments and investment properties will fill with stinking silt, their white edifices lined with impossible-to-get-out stains, marking the slowly receding water level.

There must be other people in the area with a memory. Surely it must occur to someone down by the river that the old houses were built on stilts for a reason. You only need to take a drive to the hinterland to see flood markers telling you the bridge you are about to cross can be six feet under. It's not that hard to imagine what a disaster that much water would create downstream.

Apparently, a megadam is to be built just north of us, at Traveston Crossing. A knee-jerk reaction to the drought, it will flood the Mary River basin, some of the most fertile farmland in the region, to ensure future supply to the projected population growth of Brisbane.

Some desperate public servant, in an effort to keep his contracted job, has consulted a rainfall map, noticed the little green spot of slightly higher average rainfall just west of Fraser Island — and suddenly, X marks the spot! Maybe the dam will fill to capacity some day. Maybe it will eventually rain like it did in 1974, and 1989, when a year's rain fell in one month, but it's a long time between drinks. I, for one, am glad I won't have to rely on it for my water supply. Let the projected-population real estate buyer beware!

I recall half-forgotten stories about humidity, and the sights and sounds that link it to climate. My grandmother was certain that ant action round the sink means rain is on the way, and that the squalling and screeching of yellow-tailed black-cockatoos heralds a change.

Why on Earth did it never occur to anyone to ask the original locals all this stuff before we made them forget it? The Gubbi Gubbi people, whose collective memory could stretch back for countless generations, must have recorded climatic patterns and seasonal fluctuations in their song cycles. Imagine what has been lost by disruption of their language and culture, all that wisdom and knowledge swept away by us ignorant invaders with our 'superior' Western logic, empirical science and bald-faced greed.

All I have is a record of the last hundred years of rainfall for this area, and nothing but an extrapolated

statistical probability of what may happen tomorrow —
about as reliable as hope.

But for now, thankfully, tomorrow is here. Leaden cloud
has descended into the valley. It's raining, full on, no let-
up for the past two days and I feel like Mrs Noah
confined to the ark. Geoffrey comes to the door in
raincoat and gumboots and announces: 'I think we're
going under!' The place, he says, has turned into a coral
reef overnight: outside, in the leaf mould, on the
compost heap, sprouting from dead tree limbs and the
garden paths, are every conceivable shape of fungus and
mushroom. Some mimic flowers, some resemble starfish,
or sport frilly tentacles like a sea anemone. Amazing!

I am weightless in a huge ocean of wet air, like a fish
shoaling around in the shallows, confined to the oxygen-
concentrated layer of moisture that its gills can process.
But we humans don't have the freedom of a fish. We're
forever stuck on the seabed, more like a tube worm that's
graduated to hermit crab, all pink and fleshy and
vulnerable. We scuttle from carapace to empty carapace
in our bottom-feeding existence, constructing brilliantly
luminescent glittering reefs of concrete and glass to cling
to, and though we've found ways to mimic fish, we're
always going to be stuck here between the devil and the

deep blue sea, as clouds pile up above like breakers ruffling the surface of unfathomable blue ether. You get that in the country — everything is so much bigger than it looks on TV.

The saltless tide is in again, flooding the rock pool of our valley, gushing into its sunbaked ceramic basin, pouring down the overflows. Green fuzz blooms on furniture and leather and the smell of wet earth and damp and rot rises up from the ground. Within days, the hillsides are glazed celadon and emerald and the two-month-old calves are confused and delighted by the slipping and sliding muddiness of their play.

And our tank is filling up.

Winter

3rd June

Rainfall last month: almost 3 inches!

Jobs for this month:

- Sow — 8th, 9th or 10th: broad beans. 17th & 18th: Chioggia beetroot. 26th & 27th: Ruby Red chard, Vertus cabbage, Tall Utah celery, dill, Green Sprouting Calebrese broccoli, Roi de Carouby snow peas.
- Move chooks onto beds 5 & 6, front garden; sow with green manure.
- Pot out winter seedlings.
- Gather kindling & firewood; stack and dry logs.
- Lay in mulch.
- Install new stove.
- Get a job.

I am the mother of creation.

I've got a red plastic toolbox that contains all the stuff I need to sustain life: seeds. The box once contained all my drawing materials, but they produce only a pale imitation of this other life — real life, as opposed to still-life. In my red toolbox is a collection as precious as any art collection. Whereas pictures are two-dimensional representations of three, my seeds are perfectly compact four-dimensional holograms. A whole material existence over time is encoded in them. I hold these minuscule containers of becoming in my hand and wonder:

How do they know what to be?

How can all that complexity be contained in these time capsules? Their imagination is astonishing. You wouldn't think there could possibly be enough room in there for a mind, but they must have one, with one all-pervading purpose: to imagine and replicate themselves in spectacular detail. Seeds cannot be mere dumb, stupid matter — there is mysterious intelligence lurking in the tiny mind of a plant.

I've been slowly depositing into my seed bank from a catalogue published by the aptly named Eden Seeds. They grow a range of organic old-traditional, open-pollenated varieties of vegetables, herbs and flowers that you'll never see fruiting on the shelves of the supermarket, and would test Adam's inventiveness in naming. The variety is wondrous: fifty kinds of beans, for starters, in a range of shades of blossom and pod colours — Purple Kings, magic beans which turn from purple to deep green when cooked; Scarlet Runners, which ramble over my shade house and set it on fire with their carmine bloom for at least seven years of perennial re-shooting.

I had no idea about this kaleidoscopic diversity. I am now devoted to discovering the beauty of all these expressions of form. Each couple of months, I splurge on a few exotic heirlooms and try them out.

Heirlooms are plant varieties passed down through generations of growers, much like Grandma's jewellery, but much more precious. The mass production and selective breeding of modern cultivars has seen the gradual erosion of genetic diversity.

Heirlooms are insurance against this loss, and one day may actually be the only thing that stands between feast and widespread, large-scale famine — a vital bank of pest- and disease-resistant seed stock.

By growing them in my own garden, I am adding to the diversity, as the varieties I plant adapt themselves to the conditions here.

And to think, only a year or two ago I couldn't distinguish between brassica and lettuce seedlings. Now, at the emergence of the first true leaf, I can differentiate cabbage and broccoli.

Beetroots are not only red. They come in yellow, white and, believe it or not, red-and-white layers that look like bull's-eyes when they are cut in half. There are chocolate-coloured capsicums; little squat, round carrots;

and corn with multicoloured red, blue and white kernels. And kale! I'd never heard of it before, with its curly ruffles of blue or red. And watermelons are not just pink inside, they can be yellow or orange, and the patterning on their skins can range to deep dark green with veridian stripes or patches and spots of lemon yellow.

My dad worked in the fruit and vegetable industry. He was a merchant, and every year we went with him to North Queensland for melon season over the last three months of the school year. Some mornings, long before sunrise, Mum dug us out of bed and bundled us up in the back of the car to follow Dad out to load. He'd have organised half a dozen semis and most of the local moonlighting police force to arrive at a paddock by 4 am. There was no such thing as childcare; we went with our parents to help. Light and slender, we kids could scatter straw high up in the load without bruising the fruit. Each melon was tossed, hand to hand, along a line of men, from piles in the field, up to the truckie, who tenderly laid each one down, row after row, on our straw bedding. He knew that if he was slack about it his load would be leaking, fermented and putrid, through the planks of his flat-back trailer before he made it to the Sydney markets.

The vague whiff of discarded fruit rotting in the already-hot morning sun accompanied our breakfast of freshly dropped melons. The first taste of watermelon season always brings that stink back to mind — and consequently I'm not a fan, but I love the surprise of the fruit swelling, appearing almost overnight under filigreed vine leaves. And the Coven loves them.

The markets back then were pretty basic — staple vegetables of green, orange and white, stone fruit, apples and citrus, and that was about it. It was still a seasonal activity. We knew Christmas was close when Dad arrived home in the afternoon, stomping a little more heavily up the back stairs, weighed down by a case balanced on his shoulder: cherries, blushing pink mangoes from Bowen, or big fuzzy peaches. We lived in a permanent state of abundance, and I loved to go to the markets with him, to get caught up in the frenetic energy of the place. The colour and movement of men loading trucks, women sorting and trimming cabbages and cauliflowers or, like my aunty, picking through boxes of tomatoes for stung fruit. The dust and piles of rotting greens filled my small consciousness with a sensuality I'd almost forgotten till now.

I remember the speculation about whether or not to deal in avocados, a new, wildly exotic addition to the market stock. Nanna wouldn't touch them — 'poor man's butter', she called them — they made her gag on bitter memories of the Depression, and when eggplant and zucchinis first appeared: *Foreign muck*. She stubbornly stuck to her Anglo meat-and-three-veg.

Dad had left the business by the time Woolworths started dealing direct with growers, putting them on contract and cutting out the middleman. Slowly, more and more lines crept in. Glasshoused out-of-season crops appeared, to meet demand for uniform, unblemished produce all year round. Then, with a growing import market made possible by lower-cost air freight, the seasons soon lost their characteristic flavour.

But here, in my garden, the seasons are tasty again. This month I will plant out my cooler-weather seedlings, and can hardly contain my desire for raw snow peas — Roi de Carouby this year, which, the catalogue tells me, is a climber with 'long thick succulent pods and deep purple flowers'. I'm hanging out for broad beans braised in butter with black pepper, the sharp frizz of curly endive, and the velvety delight of creamy cauliflower cheese. There is no comparison with these pleasures from the garden, only three months away.

I'm still having some trouble (well a lot, actually) getting my head around the fourth dimension of this gardening thing, timing it so that seedlings are large enough to plant out just as the chooks move on. Their dome moves every fortnight, but according to my moon chart, there is only one optimum time each month to sow leafy greens, fruiting annuals and root vegetables into the well-fertilised plot they've left.

I've taken to planting by the moon, which, although it sounds totally woo-woo to my once rigidly sceptical instincts, actually works. I have a calendar that tells me when the moon passes through the most favourable star signs for planting. It also points out the best phase of the moon in which to prune or fertilise and irrigate, based on the idea that the first two phases favour above-the-ground plant activity, the third favours root formation and the fourth is for doing anything that doesn't involve planting — like harvesting, making compost, weeding, mowing, or lying about reading with a vodka and tonic to hand. The calendar also notes in minute detail specific days when it's not advisable to do anything at all. I had absolutely no idea about any of this stuff; the calendar gave me somewhere to start. More often than not, when the calendar tells me to plant, it will rain, or will at least be overcast, giving seedlings a chance of surviving their transplant. It's uncannily accurate, which isn't so surprising when you consider that lunar planting is the distillation of countless generations of observation. In reality, very scientific!

Apart from the calendar providing a structure around which to organise all the tasks that need to be done to keep the whole system ticking over, it's made me aware of the moon herself — I never noticed her in the city. Now, having followed her passage for the past two years, I'm slowly getting the hang of knowing what that heavenly body is up to.

We get a lot of moon out here. If I climb the steep eastern ridge I can watch her emerge from the horizon, her shiny body veiled in blushing pink, which gradually falls away to reveal her lustrous gleam. Her face changes over the seasons: sometimes a woman, sometimes a toothless grinning child, and at others a rabbit. (They may have touched down on her perfect body, but I just can't imagine a man in the moon.)

Over the moon cycle is laid the rotation of the chooks. Every fortnight for three months, the Coven clear and fertilise each of the six circular beds, which are the same size as the base of their dome, and just as soon as they move, the beds are planted with the seedlings I have sprouted and potted out the previous month. Theoretically, three months later the plants will mature every two weeks, so I'll have a constant and varied supply of vegetables, with a subsequent planting the following three months, which will provide the Coven with greens to eat when they return for the next circuit, following their spin around the six front-garden beds, six months later. This is, unfortunately, much easier said than done. There are setbacks.

During my first attempt at this method of gardening, I battled to get seedlings up before they were devoured, every last one, by at least one very hungry mouse. Keeping poultry means grain, and grain means mice and rats, who appear to like their cereal with a side salad of my sprouts. They put back planting three months. But when they moved into the house, my live-and-let-live philosophy went out the window. It's Ratsak till the carpet snakes wake up and get back on duty.

And bandicoots. Bandicoots dig enormous divots in freshly planted beds and, although not interested in the seedlings, can in one night devastate a whole afternoon's work in their quest for insects and worms. I wish they ate mice.

I know all this seems more complex than the Mayan calendar, with coinciding cogs of moon and planting cycles, but I've given myself over to its patterning, and everything else I do is planned to fit its rhythm. Before this discipline was imposed on my days, time here was a desert. I kept losing track of it. Hours seemed to evaporate, whole days and weeks — there one minute and gone the next. I was completely unable even to keep track of what day it was. The further away I got from the mechanical measures of time — clocks and watches and deadlines and the like — the more it felt like I was outside time, or rather, that it was inside me, as vital as breathing.

It passes in waves, time. Elastic and supple, it kisses and penetrates my existence in this valley. Here there is time to remain held by moonlight animating a silver-gelatin landscape, or the passage of the guinea fowl round and round the house, enclosing us in a circle of joyous *doo-dee-ootling* energy. An hour in the garden can go on for months at a time as I stand there, silent, imagining the size and shape a seedling will take on maturity and deciding where to place it in the bed, sculpting future form.

I'm beginning to understand what it means to be a four-dimensional being, to be able to project one's imagination and will into a wide expanse of time. It's no longer a linear concept for me, but rather spreads out in all directions like an ocean, pacific or violent with tides, eddies and turbulence.

For the first time in my life since childhood I have the space to dream, to be awake but in a dreaming state of wonder, and I find myself trying to imagine the answers to a few basic questions: where do I come from, what am I doing here, and where am I going? In the city the answers were: Sydney, work and the Bayswater Brasserie, but here those questions lead me to a much-expanded outer and inner universe. They lead my gaze up into the clouds whose fleeting images are cast and caught in my imagination, or into my garden to regard small things and adjust my view to the microcosmos. There, I open a dusty envelope of memory containing all my comprehension of beauty, geometry, mythology and art and literature, in order to examine the face of a sunflower:

Man that is born of woman hath but a short time to live
and is full of misery
He cometh up and is cut down,
like a flower.

I can't help thinking that the word 'misery' should actually be 'mystery', because what a piece of work we both are. The sunflower and I share the same urge to live, and every cell of our matter contains all the genetic information our material being needs to express our perfect form in time. The sunflower knows what it is, and keeps striving towards that aim: during a three-month packet of time it becomes itself, then the head unfolds a spectacular display of petals to expose its astonishing geometric wheels of seed. Afterwards, the flower droops and declines.

Likewise, I know what I am. I've done the spectacular sexual display and seeding thing, but I've still got a bit more time on my hands before I hit the compost heap, and I get to spend a lot of it thinking. Out here in the midst of plenty of time, thoughts breed other thoughts, ideas arrive like bees. While I acknowledge the loss of the hive-heat of the city, it has been a pleasure to slow down enough to relax; become rooted in my garden. We swore off TV years ago, and the lack of its incessant chatter frees us to listen to the radio, dig into my library of unread books, listen to music, and generate ideas of my own.

This space–time thing has led me through some pretty weird reading, about physics and sacred geometry, and the correlations between ratios of sound, form and harmonics, waves and cycles. I even went out and bought myself a pair of compasses, and obsessively tried to work out how to picture the relationships. I remember learning all this stuff at primary school: intersecting circles, working out phi with a piece of string, trying to fathom the magic of the 'golden mean' — never dreaming that there is a whole mystical, philosophical basis to it. Now I'm beginning to understand why teachers thought it important enough to bore little children with. If only they'd provided the whole story.

So now I have the time to indulge in utterly useless research into the nature of the universe. There is a lot to be said for gazing into the linty, puckered creases of one's navel. There would probably have been more female philosophers if they'd had as much time as the boys to engage in such activity. But I suppose someone had to get dinner.

In Sydney I'd almost stopped cooking altogether. Never had enough time, and the warehouse studio wasn't really set up for domesticity. We had an electric kettle and frypan, a microwave and bar fridge, and no plumbing from the sink. Waste water drained into a bucket which had to be emptied into the toilet on the other side of the building. Our occupancy in the warehouse was kind of illicit, no one was supposed to be living there, but as we were prepared to compromise and get around the small problem of creature comforts, we were able to enjoy the pleasure of wallowing about in the golden afternoon light that flooded in through a bank of enormous sash windows, and the beautiful resonance of those capacious wooden-floored spaces.

I did miss the pleasure of practising that most intimate of art forms and would occasionally do a roast in the frypan, but it was a difficult thing to achieve in the circumstances. In an effort to insult me, my adorable son, more attached to creature comforts than I, and appalled by the lack of basic plumbing, exclaimed one afternoon, 'Mum, how can you live in this' — searching for the word and getting it wrong — 'bohemian paradise!' Out of the mouths of babes.

But up here I cook. It is my daily ritual of love. Tonight we're having soup, because we've stopped eating large evening meals. After a day on the tractor out in the sun, Geoffrey tends to fall over with a resounding thud if we indulge in excesses of pot-roasted lamb with juniper berries, neck of pork braised in milk, spuds baked in butter and cream, or even puddings, pies and home-made bread. So we are dining like paupers these days, on soups containing whatever vegetable is in the garden at the time (and my bum is beginning to resume human proportions!). All I need keep on hand is butter, a few basic groceries and a supply of onions, the only thing I don't grow. They just don't do well here for some reason. At the moment I've got gallons of stock — wallaby stock …

Almost home, dusk, beautiful evening with spectacular sky, and *wham* — didn't see her till she was right in front of the car, then under it, taking out the new exhaust-system Geoffrey had just installed. I got out to look back up the road for missing car parts and spied an object about twenty yards away. Going closer I found it was a joey — all pink and hairless, eyes fused but still alive. I picked it up off the road, cupped its tininess in one hand, and looked back to see Geoffrey gathering up the hefty weight of the mother. She seemed to be much heavier than she looked.

As I walked back to the car, I thought about the times in the last two years I'd dodged Skippy (we call them all Skippy) on the drive up the hill. The wallabies here are a small breed with delicate black-dipped paws and fuzzy coppery-grey fur, and they've become accustomed to us. There's been two generations born since we moved in, and this mother would have been a joey herself not that long ago.

Geoffrey had the car going and reckoned he could nurse it the couple of miles to the house. In the dim glow of the interior light I could see the extent of the baby's head injuries. There was no way to save it, so rather than let it suffer any longer, I wrung its neck, shed tears, and kept its little body for the compost. I suggested that perhaps we do the same with the mother's body, but as I climbed into the passenger side I realised that Geoffrey was a step ahead of me. He had already put the dead doe on the floor at my feet.

It's dangerous to leave a carcass on the road for other creatures to find. Eagles have learned that road kill is an easy dinner, and often end up as road kill themselves defending it. This death wouldn't be such a waste if we took her back to compost — but on the way home with her still-warm body pressing on my bare ankles, it occurred to me that she'd been killed instantly with no trauma and no adrenalin in her system to sour the meat. I decided to butcher her.

I had never butchered anything larger than a chicken before. We hung her up under the house, fetched knives and basins, and I rehearsed the process in my head. It had to be done immediately — we have no coldroom, and though it's cool at night, even in June the days are still hot and flyblown. I had a vague notion that a carcass should be hung to let the blood drain away before skinning. So I made the first cut at her throat, then found myself strangely fascinated by the misty stream of hot liquid leaking from the wound, dripping into the metal basin below.

I'd seen whole hides at art school, the jagged six-pointed star shape of tanned leather before it is cut and sewn into shoes and coats, and managed now to figure out where the cuts should be to get the skin off in one piece. So, I set about flaying her, my concentration focused only on the difficult task in my hands. It wasn't till the last of her pelt parted from her flesh that I pulled back — shocked, confronted by the charnel reality of what I was doing.

Her body was now stripped of the clothing of her species, naked, reduced to the matter of its mammalian form — meat. I've handled cold mountains of meat over a lifetime of carnivorous consumption, all neat and hygienically arranged in the butcher's counter window, garnished with sprigs of plastic parsley. But I had no inkling of how difficult it would be to slice into warm flesh, still slippery and formless as jelly.

I suppose it is their size that allows us to feel sufficiently distanced from chickens and fish, their bodies are so much smaller, and their flesh is white, and I can kid myself that it's somehow karma-neutral. But a big animal, heavy as oneself, is a whole other kettle of stock. I wonder how hungry I'd need to be before I could kill one of our calves with my own hands, and can begin to understand why the cow is sacred, why such ceremony is attached to their slaughter in other, less 'sanitised' cultures. Halal meat makes new sense to me — if you are going to eat an animal, it should be devotional, not merely habitual.

Some hours and considerable sweat later, the poor dead wallaby was transformed into a stockpot of bones and trimmings, and half a dozen, tightly Glad-Wrapped joints of meat that will age in the refrigerator. Whatever meat workers want in return for their labour is worth it. Slaughter is a laborious, blood-soaking, soul-staining business, and I will never shop for meat in the same way again. The meals we make of this wallaby will be the most expensive I'll ever prepare, because I know their real cost.

* * *

We were down in town yesterday doing the week's shopping. There's not much to town — a supermarket, hardware store, fruit shop, a couple of cafes, banks, real estate agent, a two-dollar shop and that's about it, apart from the bottle shop. I was standing outside the supermarket waiting for Geoffrey, idly reading the noticeboard where goods and services are traded, sometimes for money, sometimes for other tender, like a slab of beer, or just straight swaps, none of which passes through the national accounting system, and I saw:

For sale: wood-fired Rayburn cooker.

When Geoffrey returned, I pointed to it: 'What do you reckon?' We've been thinking, for a while now, about switching to wood for cooking and hot water, as well as heat. We have hillsides of pruning and thinning from the trees, so we're not likely to run out of firewood any time soon. I tore off a little strip of phone-numbered paper and we arranged to drive over and check it out. Its owner lives some way from town, down a dirt track, and as we turned into the driveway, it became obvious why he was switching to gas. There wasn't a stick of timber standing on his once-bush block. He'd run out of fuel for the stove.

The cooker is in fairly dodgy nick, the firebricks need replacing and there is a big crack running across the top of the oven, but it looks fixable, so now it stands forlorn on the open landing outside my kitchen, waiting till Geoffrey fits out its new home there. He's putting in doors to close the alcove off from the wildlife — mud wasps, spiders, snakes and lizards — and meanwhile he has begun gathering and drying wood to feed the stove. He promises to keep me supplied with appropriately sized sticks for the firebox, so I'm prepared to learn the art of cooking with unpredictable temperatures.

My great-aunt in Stanthorpe had a wood stove. Her kettle was permanently just moments off the boil, and outside the kitchen in the crunchy frosty morning was a woodpile, carefully stacked and labelled:

Scones, Roasts, Biscuits.

I now have the rest of my life, though I hope it won't take quite that long, to work out which wood is for what use. Intense but fast-burning wattle for cakes? Steady long-burning hardwood for roast potatoes?

The added bonus is that the stove can produce gallons of hot water, heated by a jacket behind the firebox, feeding into a big silver storage tank beside it. On the upside, the house will be toasty all over, and not just in the front room where the fireplace is. I'll be able to work at my computer without being wrapped in a doona. But on the downside, it might prove to be a furnace for the other nine months, when it's hot enough to fry eggs in the shade. But it will remain separate from the rest of the house, and Geoffrey's two new big doors will open out to theoretically suck out the excess heat.

Until it's repaired and cleaned up and chimneyed and plumbed in, I'm still paying the power bill. And until I've dreamed up a way of having the power to wean myself off the grid completely, I have to trade some of my valuable time for money to purchase pumping rights to its stream of addictive energy. All my measures towards self-sufficiency would be great if I were Prince Charles and had twenty or so people to do the actual work it takes to run an organic farm, but we are a couple of middle-aged people without a vast personal fortune. As much as I want to cut down on consumption and shed a couple of sizes from our carbon footprint, things still cost. The stove has dug a big hole in our savings, and we still can't avoid fuel, power or tax bills.

So, I've bitten the bullet, given away my silly childish dreams of living the self-sustaining, greenie-hippie-arty life, and got myself a job.

I've been offered and accepted a casual teaching contract, replacing a performing arts teacher while she is on maternity leave. There's a few weeks left till the end of term. I'm finishing off her music units, then in the new term I will be planning all the units, for Years 1 to 10, for the rest of the year.

Back to timetables and deadlines and knowing what day it is. My hermitage is over. I've had to retrieve the capacity to compartmentalise my thoughts, remember to wear a bra, and reconnect with the larger world of people and geography. Two days a week, I drive to a small country town about forty miles away, over the range to the west. That is as much time as I'm prepared to give up for goods and services.

The real cost of living is time. We trade our time for enough money to pay someone else for theirs. To maintain a relatively healthy body, I need fresh air every moment, clear water and food every day, and shelter at least half the time, to have somewhere safe to dream. There's a balance sheet in my head of how much time we've got, and how much we need to spend to purchase the necessities to sustain another day's worth of time in which to live. My idea of living is spending my time in my own domain, so sacrifices have to be made. It means drastic cuts in the entertainment budget, like choosing the cheap vodka and cask wine, no restaurant dining, no aimless shopping. But home provides me with most of the entertainment I need. We are now very good at entertaining ourselves and each other.

Tonight Geoffrey is wrapping potatoes in foil to cook in the fireplace in the living room. I'm stirring our pauper's feast: carrot soup, adding up its real cost in my head, running the account of the time it has taken to get us to this point in time:

- Ten years for the giant old wattle to die and fall over in the top paddock.
- A week to cut enough off it for winter, and move it out of the weather to the house.
- A couple of months to dry it.
- Two years to get the garden soil friable and fertile.
- Three months to grow the vegetables.
- Half an hour to pick, wash, and prepare them for the pot.
- A moment to switch on the hotplate and a few more for it to heat up.
- A couple of hours working for money to fund the power use, and buy the foil and onions and butter, and fuel for the chainsaw.
- An instant to accidentally kill the wallaby.
- Five hours to butcher her and another few to make the stock from her bones.
- A quarter of an hour to build the fire and two hours to let it die down to coals to cook the potatoes.

In twenty minutes dinner will be on the table, steaming, composed of all the concentrated time and energy it took to prepare — just enough to get us through till tomorrow morning when we'll breakfast, courtesy of the Coven. Everything Geoffrey and I consume is shared. Consequently, he and I are now made of the same matter, combusting at the same intensity on the same fuel.

I have never felt closer to another human, apart from Evan, my son, made of my own flesh; but as his manhood draws him away from me, Geoffrey burns brighter. We not only fuel our bodies with the same food, but feed our minds with the same books and fill our hearts with the same sensual delights of our existence. Now I know why, after the Fall, Eve had to take Adam with her, and why he went — they shared the same being.

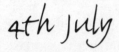

4th July

Rainfall last month: three and a half inches

Jobs for this month:

- Sow — 6th & 7th: Tropic tomatoes, Marconi Red capsicum, Casper eggplant. 14th & 15th: Thumbelina carrots, golden beets, Carentan leeks. 30th & 31st: broccoli, basil, Vertus cabbage, Tendercrisp celery, Mignonette lettuce, parsley, Brown Romaine silverbeet.
- Harvest corn & last of peas on bed 4, take down trellises.
- Move chooks to back garden (need help cross-country).
- Plant out beds 1 & 2, winter crops.
- Pull snake-bean bed, compost & mulch side bed 4.
- Dig out mouse traps — carpet snakes are dormant.
- Brush up on keyboard & learn infant songs.
- Prepare for middle school term 3 unit.

The sun is getting up later these days. I tend to sleep till it is snuggled up in the room with me and can tempt me out from under the covers into the fresh morning air. Geoffrey considerately resists turning the radio on till

I'm fully awake, with his cup of morning coffee in my hand. The news of the world has been so bad lately that if I take the information in before fully conscious, I stay angry and irritable for the whole day.

When he does turn the radio up, I hear that today's theme is Independence — all fireworks and celebration, and I'm wondering why I need to care about this foreign holiday, and why I'm hearing nothing but a cracked American accent cackling over my airwaves, bleating about freedom and democracy and blathering on about nationhood and patriotic fervour for the war on terror, as if it's some party I've been invited to. Haven't we got a big enough flag of our own to wave, or enough of our own national myths to shore up with props of hollow sentiment and omissions of truth? Like Anzac Day, that quaint ritual which in Australia surpasses any religious festival. It was once a heartfelt remembrance of sacrifice, tragedy and loss, but has now been hijacked by conservative spinners to gee everybody up into a state of anticipated glory in war in the Middle East …

See, ranting already, and it's only 6.30 am!

Last Anzac Day, Geoffrey found our pet birds, slaughtered. I'd raised them all from chicks and hadn't been able to eat them, so they were given names and grew personalities. I know this is difficult to imagine of two chooks, a rooster and a turkey, but they were adorable in their own particular ways. Old Peck was a white-meat bird who had way outlived her use-by date. She had dreadful, old lady's feet with swollen arthritic ankles, no feathers on her belly because she was so fat it dragged along the ground, and a disgusting daggy arse, out of which, miraculously, fell one perfect egg every couple of days. She was not bred for her reproductive capacity and, I suspect, went into lay when the last of her kin got the chop as a means of avoiding the same fate.

I came to believe that she was the incarnation of my favourite nanna. They had a lot in common, not least of which was Old Peck's cluck of righteous indignation and moral outrage when I introduced a flock of younger birds into her pen. Among them was Mick, a young bantam rooster who was to become the Coven's boyfriend, and a little bantam hen I'd hoped would go clucky and hatch a new flock of layers for me. Then there was Peckaturk, a stupid big palooka of a juvenile turkey.

Peckaturk had had a twin who fell prey to the resident carpet snake, but when they were little poults, they did everything in such elegant unison that they became known as the Turkish ballet, and looked the part too, right down to their pink-stockinged legs, fluffy feathered tutus and delicate, wary-stepped flightiness. When I put them in with Old Peck, they appointed her their mother and, much to her horror, followed her round relentlessly, trying to park their comparatively large selves underneath hers.

Most people think turkeys are dead ugly, but I thought Peckaturk among the most beautiful of feathered creatures. Sure, he was adolescently ungainly, had your average case of teenage spots, lumps and a fairly obvious Adam's apple, but he had the most beautiful innocent eye: quizzical, pensive and sentient. Peckaturk was all soul — completely ethereal. He'd fallen desperately in love with Geoffrey, and when he fluffed up and ruffled his feathers in amorous display for him, I heard the sifting of angel wings.

I had dreamed of the demise of his brother, the other little avian ballerina. I remember quite clearly in the dream, telling the flock that no, they couldn't have the rather attractive curtain they'd hung in front of their house, instead of being locked in at night — but they insisted, and I saw the snake slide in just as I'd warned. Then, a couple of days before the massacre, I dreamed of a pack of feral dogs under our house, which confronted me. It was one of those nightmare moments when you want to scream out for help but can't. One of the dogs had two heads — one normal and one meaty, hairless and festering. I didn't think anything more of it, assuming it had something to do with all the alchemical symbolism I'd been immersed in while looking into the nature of matter.

It's very strange being out here in the midst of nature. If I'd had those dreams in Sydney, I'd have had to assume that they had some deep Jungian symbolism; but here, everything I dream is in direct relationship to the immediate environment. Perhaps dreams aren't really symbolism. Perhaps we dream realities, past, present and future. Somewhere, some time, the innocents are being slaughtered by the dogs of hell, and we are all witness to it. And I refuse to believe that animals do not know that they die. If so, why then was the chook pen strewn with feathers? If Peckaturk didn't know he was about to be killed, why did he put up such a fight to survive? Humans are so ignorant about the consciousness of other creatures. We assume that they don't know that they are doomed, as we do, but how can we possibly know for sure? After all, we appear outwardly calm even though aware of *our* mortality!

The image of their feathers spread all over the yard and the idea of their bodies torn to pieces still breaks my heart. Geoffrey spared me the actual crime scene, gathering up their body parts and burying them in the compost heap before I got out of bed. But it made me think about all the innocents caught in the jaws of their helplessness. Imagine if you came home to such a sight but instead of chickens it was your children, your family all murdered on the lawn. Suddenly I comprehended the emotion of Macduff's speech in the Scottish play: *What, all my pretty chickens and their dam, in one fell swoop?*

That evening, still mourning poor Peckaturk and all my pretty chickens, I was in Iraq even though I was only at my computer, reading the words of Riverbend, who has been blogging since the war began. And a year later, I am still reading the same blog. She is a young Iraqi woman, middle class, articulate and a gifted writer in English. She speaks from the domestic front line of the war, about electricity rationing, lack of petrol, increasing violence, sham politics and, most vividly, about the slaughter of innocents, and of relatives and friends suffering.

Perhaps it is her reality I dream here, in the antipodes to her waking life. While she wakes in hell, I dream the two-headed-dog horror of it. I am responsible, as responsible as I was for the death of my birds. We left their door open on the night of the massacre, just as we left the political door open for our dog of a government to do the bidding of its master, and let it loose to leap at the throats of Iraq's innocents. I hope that while I am awake, my cosseted, comfortable, abundant, peaceful existence fills Riverbend's dreams. It's the least I can do but it falls seriously short of the best I can do.

Somehow, the Coven survived the attack. Perhaps it was because Mick had the courage or stupidity to get down off the perch to protect the girls. The only thing left of him was a handful of his beautiful iridescent black–green tail feathers. Or maybe the Coven frightened the living daylights out of their assailants. Chickens can be vicious.

It was never pretty watching the original Coven sort itself out. Of the six founding members, Hen Linda was first to come into lay, but it soon became obvious that there was a pitched battle going on between pullets Jane and Burridge for top dog. Poor pullets Rachel and Ali seemed a bit startled by the whole thing and everybody took it out on diminutive Barnsey. Things eventually settled down when they all came into lay, and final rank was established.

Hen Burridge, the benign overlord and highest ranking official, never deigned to actually do any of the dirty work. She delegated to Hen Jane, and whenever Barnsey overstepped the rules of warfare, Jane had to go in and sort her out by taking a slice of her bruised and shredded comb. Hens Linda, Rachel and Ali were of equal rank, and all, sadly, hen-pecked Barnsey, who became nervy and ratty, but laid the largest eggs for some unknown reason.

In fact, they all have their own little personality traits. Ali still likes to jump up at the mouth of the cage, flap up to my shoulder and nuzzle up, her feathers sun-warmed and soft against my cheek. Hen Linda is the conciliator — if Barnsey is copping it, Linda sits beside her in commiseration and pecks bits of chaff off her back.

Chickens are also racist. When I put four new pullets into the dome, the mottled tan and white Coven only picked on poor Four and Twenty, the black birds. The unfortunately coloured ones were too terrified to come downstairs from the perch, and at night were too afraid to stay there because Mando, one of the other newbies, had taken to relentlessly plucking all the feathers from their nether regions till they bled. I found myself patching them up with vaseline so the others didn't savage them in a frenzy of blood lust.

They have settled down into a bit of a routine now, in which the new girls spend all day upstairs wishing they had the courage to flap down and make a break for food, but have to wait till it's time for the Coven's beauty sleep to make the most of the few remaining moments of daylight and guts down whatever leftovers remain, before retiring in the laying box.

Finally, neurotic Barnsey fell off the perch. Perhaps it was exhaustion — she never let up her harassment of the new girls. I'd hear them squabbling from the bathroom window and look out to see Barnsey latched Rottweiler-like onto one of the black hen's combs, being dragged along by the terrified victim who'd already grown much bigger than her. I'd rush out to separate them and sit in the cage till everyone calmed down. With me there it was all sweetness and light, but the minute my back was turned it would be on again. Just like us humans. It's not easy being the big chicken.

I have a theory that human society has evolved from observation of poultry. Consider the number of cliches that are currently in common usage: to fly at, to be cooped up, to fly the coop, the pecking order, to shake one's tail feather, to rule the roost, to put all your eggs in one basket, to carry on like a chook with its head cut off, to get cocky, to scratch around, to be henpecked, and to fall off the perch!

All this can be applied especially to the behaviour of young teenagers. Their pecking order is as complex and vicious as the Coven's — and I am about to start term three, to move among Years 8 and 9 as the big chicken, and hang on to that lofty perch for dear life.

★   ★   ★

It's only two days a week, but it feels like more. The drive takes three-quarters of an hour. I have to be on the road by 7.30 am or I may not make the bell, because there are inevitably either roadworks or dairy cattle on their way back from milking, who take their time and are not at all perturbed by cars. The drive itself, however, is lovely. On fine days I take the back road that follows a winding ridge, which narrows to only the width of the road about halfway along. From there I can see down into the two rolling valleys on either side. The road twists and turns a little treacherously, but I am getting used to knowing where I'll pass the two school buses coming the other way on their route into town, and I remember to brake at the top of a hairpin plunge down onto the flats, at the end of the spur. I turn into a road hung with eerie signs nailed up high in the eucalypts:

Dam Level, or *Dam Buffer Zone*.

It is unnerving to imagine all this countryside under water, most of which will only be about three feet deep, as far as I can tell. Such a waste. The locals aren't giving up without a fight, though. I can't think how rabidly feral I'd become if I'd received one of those official Queensland Government letters of expulsion from Eden.

At the school I've discovered that many of the students and teachers live in the proposed catchment. One woman on staff is constantly in tears at the thought of having to move — forty years it has taken them to build their farm, and she is completely devastated. One little kid missed school because the family went on a trip to the city to find somewhere new to live and work. He came back excited with stories of Maccas on every corner and was obviously stunned by the size and density of the big smoke, but they'll never be able to find anything like the life they lead out here in the sticks, certainly not for the same money. The callousness of the government in forcing the relocation of these people is scary. And the school will lose a teacher when the enrolment numbers inevitably fall, so everyone, staff and students, is ratty and anxious about the future.

By the turn onto the main road I light my last cigarette for the morning, and can just finish it before I sweep into the town's main drag, swing through the school gates and pull up, shagged from the drive, but ready for the front line.

Staffroom, coffee, pigeonhole, quick hellos to staff, photocopying, rush to the room to assess previous damage — it's a multi-use space — rearrange furniture, rub dumb graffiti off the whiteboard — bugger, they used oil-based pen — find white spirit to clean it off, double check that timetable actually corresponds to teaching materials and lesson plans. Is the sports carnival on this week or next week? Phew, ready, bring it on.

First up this morning is middle school drama, a group of loud, unruly, out-there, confident, naive, introspective, damaged, forthright, self-conscious, insecure, emotionally conflicted, regular run-of-the-mill twelve- to fourteen-year-olds. Scary as.

Last term I'd suggested we do a unit of drama next. The usually blank, sullen faces lit up with curiosity. They'd never done drama at school before, so I could safely assume that they'd all be starting off on the same footing, knowing nothing. They were to go away on holidays and come back with a bunch of ideas about which play we'd do. Of course, they didn't, so we get to do my choice, a brilliant three-act play for young teens.

They tumble into the room joyous and boisterous as large-pawed puppies, eventually sit down, lose the mobile phones, iPods, gum, and take a copy of the script. I ask for the confident readers to show hands. They take the larger roles and we begin. Never seen them so quiet and concentrated. They laugh at all the jokes and I can hear them getting the rhythm of it.

At first they were all just a tray of identical seedlings, but now I'm coming to know them better, I can see their true leaves forming as their personalities hesitantly emerge and express themselves. Miraculously, there are precisely the same number of characters in the play as in the group, and they all know each must play one of them. By the end of the reading they are excited and have already decided who they want to be. At least seven leading ladies. This is going to be a little bit more fraught than I thought.

And they aren't the only ones who'll be acting. I have to remember how to masquerade as an authority figure, how to feign disapproval of their extreme behaviour and somehow manage to keep my fruity language in check. I have to pretend to be the grown-up. I have the costume: greying hair and scary librarian glasses, topping off a predominantly black wardrobe. I imagine I look like an old crow of a nanna to these kids. It helps.

After lunch it's the little school — they're doing plays too. Years 3 and 4 are devising their own script, and Years 5 to 7 are doing 'published scripted drama'. I'm taking this all strictly by the book — that's *syllabus*, in teacher talk. There's no room for originality here — I'm flat out catching up on pedagogy, and I'm not even trained for primary school. I'm a high school art and English teacher. The one experience I have of teaching small children was my own son. So the only reason I could even consider taking the contract is that there was the opportunity for professional development attached to it.

It's an eye-opener. Everything has changed since I last stood before a bunch of kids and tried to teach them anything. For starters, I'm no longer a green kid myself

— I've got a whole lifetime of experiential knowledge of my subject areas; and, secondly, teachers up here are being asked to embed into their practice 'Dimensions of Learning' — an idea that suggests that if children are given the opportunity to work across a wide range of ways of learning, they will learn more efficiently and effectively. We are endeavouring to teach children *how* to think, not what to think. They learn to reason and categorise rather than mimic and memorise. Of course, you can see why the government of the day might have a problem with the idea of the next generation being able to think for itself. The kiddies might become immune to the spin-cycled language of politics and be in a position to resist the thrall of advertising, and MTV, and manufactured sentimental nationalism.

They'll have access to all the higher forms of thought that were once only available at university. When they become adults they'll be able to think beyond their mortgage, from a larger perspective; they'll know about subtext and irony, and become capable of projecting themselves beyond their experience, be able to extrapolate, to argue, to imagine and make informed judgments. They will, as a generation, have rediscovered empathy. Well, that's the plan, anyway.

School for my generation was about fear and loathing, corporal punishment and submission — now it's about care, mutual respect and personal responsibility. And it's got me hooked, even though it represents a 180-degree shift from my earlier training.

If the kids I'm teaching grow up and take with them the mode of being human that is currently being emphasised, then there is hope for Australia yet, but if they have to start putting their little hands over their hearts and swear allegiance to flags, and sing the words to that awful national anthem of ours with images of Simpson's donkey before their eyes — forget it — we're back in 1965 again, and I, for one, refuse to go there.

But it's not going to be easy. Kids who have books and the Net are up against the kids who have disaffection and dysfunction. For every kid who reads Harry Potter, there's ten who can barely read their own names. Till you get out here, in among it, you don't notice that the society you think you live in isn't the society that you actually live in at all. It's fucked out here on the edges, as it ever has been.

But worse is yet to come in my big day out in the world — after big lunch is Years 1 and 2. *Argggghhhhh!* I have absolutely no idea how to deal with five- and six-year-olds en masse. When I told my sister, who currently has one, that I was going to be teaching Year 1, she looked at me with a combination of doubt, horror, dismay and general disbelief. '*Oowah*,' she groaned, as if she'd just delivered afterbirth, *'they're wild animals!'* And she is correct.

Little kids spend much of their lives at school with their teeth bared, claws extended and fur up on their necks. They stalk each other, jealously guard their own space, and resist all attempts at socialisation. They are in no way like the biddable, calm kiddies I saw on *Sesame Street* or *Romper Room*. They have no concept of the verb *to share*, nor any individual capacity to comprehend, when I ask them all to be quiet, that this applies in any way to their own particular little isolated, autonomous self.

I remember my own infant experience quite clearly. I was the only real person there, the only one who deserved the praise, the only one who could do the sums, the most polite, the cleverest and the prettiest, and the only one that Miss Ford, in her lovely floaty blue-and-white dress, truly loved and thought worthy of approval. Of course, this reality existed only in my own mind. Every other child in that 1960s Year 1 class was prompted by their very own experience of parental devotion to assume this was the case for them too. Nothing has changed.

In the average infants class there are twenty ravenous demands for undivided attention from one, or if the school is marginally better funded, two adult parent-substitutes.

Every time I have the infants, I feel like I'm an official in a refugee camp without enough aid to go around.

The other teacher I share them with this one afternoon a week is the sport teacher — like me, a casual contractor, untrained for this age group, who approaches them with the same white-knuckled terror that I have. I know it's only one day a week, and only for thirty-five minutes at a time, and only for subject areas that no one really cares about — sport, performing arts — not readin', 'ritin' and 'rithmatic, but for that short amount of time, *we* are there, with children entrusted to the system's care, and I can't help thinking it just doesn't care enough. We do our best under the circumstances, but the circumstances are dictated by dumb things like economic bottom lines and quotas, which have nothing to do with hearts and minds.

I get through the afternoon ordeal of nursery rhymes, drama games, grazed knees, stray kicks, pinches, bites, tears and general mayhem; then it's on to the mayhem of the weekly staff meeting. This week, behaviour management is being discussed, endlessly, from different positions on the bell curve of attitude towards how to formulate a policy. By now I'm so emotionally exhausted that I'm just barely plugged in, and hoe into a salt-and-sugar-fix from the chips, lollies and cakes provided by the rostered staff. My shout is week ten — a lifetime away.

When it's eventually over, no one is apparently any the wiser, and we all head off. The kids left ages ago, except for those whose nannas clean the school grounds of an afternoon, and the teachers' kids. Smokers leap into their cars and light up as they drive off, but I have to wait for the Valiant to warm up, which takes forever because the choke is gone, thanks to the wallaby. When I finally do get to the turn-off out of town, it's 4.30 pm. I'll get home at about 5.30, if I'm lucky, because I need to stop for fuel on the way at the only servo for miles that sells the fuel that the Valiant can guzzle.

Then, finally home, I'll pour the first of about seven vodkas, to wind down enough to even think about the debrief of the day's classes I have to do so I can plan Friday's lessons. I'll probably fall sullenly to sleep at about ten. For all of this, I am paid for five hours, at about thirty-eight dollars per hour after tax, and my vehicle and petrol are not deductable. As it takes me at least double that amount of time to actually do the job, I figure I'm working for about the same as the average sixteen-year-old checkout chick.

Home, in my sanctuary at last. I go into the garden to tend the Coven, water seedlings and pull a few weeds, pick vegetables and salad for dinner, and go over the day in my head: How to solve the seven leading ladies problem? Who should be the lead in the play? How to design and make the costumes for the Years 3 and 4 play so there's no need to ask for money and time from parents who have precious little of either? How to get the Year 7 boys motivated to join in? How to cope with the paperwork? Then I come back in and defrag into Geoffrey. He gets every detail, every word, every gesture, every nuance of interaction downloaded onto his shoulders — and then, miraculously, it all doesn't seem to weigh so heavily on mine.

After a day's teaching I'm doing all the talking, but it's only because I've got so much to say. Most of the time we barely speak to each other. When we are in the same place and head-space, words don't seem necessary. I've lately also noticed that jobs I'm sure were only listed in my head are getting done, as if he is reading my mind. I'll go out to water the chooks — done. Or it occurs to me that it's beer-o'clock — he already has the glasses out and is twisting off the top of a long neck. This is very pleasing, since I have two days a week less time to attend to our real life.

Finally, I'm calmer, tucked up beside Geoffrey's fuzzy warmth, licked by the flickering glow of the fire, and we're discussing young nephew Christopher's music lesson on Saturday, in light of what I have learned today about teaching music to small children. He is in Year 1, very intelligent, and Geoffrey and I have taken on the task of teaching him music. I do the theory side of things and 'Uncle Noisy', as he is called by his sisters, looks after the fun side.

In the studio there is an ancient drum kit that Christopher loves to attack. He just goes for it while Geoffrey accompanies his performance on guitar or keyboard. Alternatively, Christopher will take to the ivories and they both go for it with a drum track playing. Geoffrey records it, plays it back with effects, and Christopher thinks that he is God. Which, of course, in that moment of unselfconscious creation, they both are. I, on the other hand, do the boring stuff. I am the mistress of the metronome, the staff and the mechanical process of showing him how noise works.

We are currently learning to play 'Puff the Magic Dragon'. Last week I found myself apologising to a five-year-old for bursting into tears — I'd suddenly become aware that, after thirty-odd years, I still haven't gotten over the Peter Pan devastation of that song's theme, which then made me realise that in spite of all best intentions, I never really ever wanted to grow up. In this valley I've found a place where I don't have to give up that wish, because here, every day, we are in the land of no plans. The 'plan' is so long-term that it is seldom impacted by the short-term. Shit happens. You deal with it. But the long-term stuff continues on about its business regardless — the trees grow, the cows drop their calves and, really, we are kind of irrelevant to it, with the exception of the occasional minor intervention. But with this teaching job, all that has changed, at least for two days a week.

I can't sleep. My head still spins, preoccupied with Friday, four days away, and a performance date four months away. Strangely, although it's got me in a turmoil, it feels kind of good to be back in the saddle — engaged and connected with the world. Poor Geoffrey, tired out from his day in the paddock and now the added emotional stress of my day at school, puts some music on in an effort to lull me.

The night is very black. Low clouds obscure the light of the new moon. I can lie in the dark with my eyes open and imagine myself in Hamlet's nutshell, adrift in infinite space. The only interruption is the pale glow of my computer's on-button, which faintly pulses a soft greenish lume from the hall.

I'm reminded of last summer's firefly.

It had somehow found its way into the room and floated up near the ceiling. Perhaps it had fallen in love with the computer light, which must represent the great mother of all fireflies. For an hour or two we lay there, listening to music, watching the amorous firefly flash its phosphorescent desire through the still darkness. Geoffrey remembered a book of Japanese haiku translations he'd read years ago — *A Net of Fireflies*. I delighted in the pun on my name.

Smiling at the thought of it, drifting, listening to Geoffrey's song, I fall eventually into sleep:

As hummingbirds anticipate sunset
clouds are slowly raining to petals.
I would be some modern-day Wendy;
'Peter take the children away please.
They don't need this fighting
and killing no more.'

Childhood'll not last forever.
Nothing's going to take us to history.
If evening sky beckons, enter.
Everybody here is believing
into pages of story woven.
Waiting as they pass by the garden.

5th August

Rainfall last month: two and a half inches

Jobs for this month:

- Sow — 3rd & 4th: Balinese corn, Tropic tomatoes, capsicum, Casper & Redskin aubergines. 11th & 12th: beetroot, leeks, Thumbelina carrots. 29th–31st: broccoli, basil, cabbage, celery, lettuce, parsley, silverbeet.
- Cover new seed house with shadecloth.
- Move chooks onto beds 3 & 4, plant out with spring crops.
- Mulch up all beds against dry weather.
- Weed front garden paths & collect bluetop flowers.
- Prepare assignments for Year 10.
- Run props & costume workshops for little-school plays.

Two more sleeps till my birthday, another year closer to my last. Better get on with it then, even though it's too cold to get out of bed because the fire has gone out and I'm rigid, and I'm getting the flu. I may feel like death warmed up, but there's still a lot to do today — chooks to be moved on, planting, and Geoffrey has spent much time and effort making a shade house at the back edge of the garden — my birthday present. One of the few advantages of being a marginally old person is that I don't have to wait till the actual day to open the loot, and in the case of this particular gift — I'll be wrapping it myself, in shadecloth.

Up until the erection of the shade house, I had nowhere to keep seedlings out of direct sunlight. I had them strategically placed under bushes, the mulberry trees, the peach tree, anything to provide shade, but it meant having to go out a couple of times a day and move them out of the creeping heat. For a while I had them on old bed frames out on the tank, the legs in tins of water, like a meat safe, so they'd be out of reach of mice. Each box was covered with a piece of shadecloth tucked snugly round its base; a row of humidicribs in a natal ward.

The new shade house is large enough to take a whole month's seedlings, and also supports a little corrugated-iron awning to catch rain and collect it in a drum I can dip into for water whenever I want, and not have to wait for the pump to be on. It has waist-high slatted shelves, and I'm so ludicrously excited by the prospect of its use, I can barely breathe, let alone wait till my actual birthday to use it. Once the shadecloth is tacked up, I'll sow the fruiting annuals I should have done yesterday. I am curious about the Casper eggplants. Imagine, white fruit! They really will be *egg* plants.

People think it's always hot on the Sunshine Coast, but up here in the hills it gets quite cold. We aren't that far above sea level — I can see it from here — but once the sun sinks below the big ghosty old *grandis* out the back at about 3 pm, the temperature drops dramatically. We even get frost sometimes, which oozes like treacle down into the flats. I've planted a sugar-cane barrier to deflect it around the edge of the garden. Although it never gets cold enough for Brussels sprouts — I've had two attempts now — other brassicas thrive in the cool, and some go above and beyond the call of duty. Broccoli are splendid in the crisp weather — deep blue with diamonds of dew collected and cupped in the folds of frilly leaves. Snow peas taste like pure rainwater first thing in the morning, their snapping crunch against teeth irresistible. I feel a whole lot better moving through my garden, thawing in the wintry sunshine.

The vitality of freshly picked food is obvious — it tastes, smells and sounds alive. I'm spoiled by it, and any leftovers are fed directly to the chooks so they can benefit from its effect on their health too. We share the produce of the garden not only with the Coven, but also the local bird and insect life. The chooks prefer their fruit teeming with maggots, and leaves covered in grubs and grasshoppers, so it's a good deal. I over-plant for our needs so there's plenty to go round. Insects only really seem to attack unhealthy plants and leave the robust prolific plants for us humans. And plants appear to have an immune system which can resist infection or infestation if they are grown in living soil, so eating them has got to be a good idea if I want the same thing for my body. This is my DIY health insurance.

It's a bit of a problem out here in the sticks, health. The local town is health oriented. They call it health, but the reality is that it is mostly engaged in the provision of death services. It's such a growth industry I even toyed with the idea of setting up as an undertaker when I moved here. People say they come north to retire, but what we are doing is dying.

The private health-care provider in town moved into what was once the base hospital. When I was a kid it served the farming and coastal communities for miles around, but now it provides the well insured with the elective extension of decrepitude. Knee and hip replacements, plastic surgery, colonoscopies, cornea repair, treatment for osteoporosis, sclerosis and diabetes — all the infirmities of old age. Noosa Hospital is the same — private, and although it is supposed to provide emergency triage for the uninsured, I don't think their heart is in it.

The year we poured the concrete pads for that fantasy holiday shed up in the top paddock, Geoffrey put a star picket though his leg. He stepped into a hole and slid down onto it, exposing all the bone of his shin. I pulled off my T-shirt, wrapped it tightly round the wound, got him into the ute and drove flat out to the local ambulance station. 'Take him down to Noosa Emergency,' they said, 'we can't fix that here — bone.' Apparently bone injuries are a worry, prone to infection. This was not making me feel any better as I drove the twenty minutes it took to pull up at Emergency.

It was Christmas, minimal staff on duty. A gaggle of people languished in the waiting room and I was panicking by now because Geoffrey had turned a whiter shade of pale, and the idea of his possible imminent demise was making me a little crazy.

Had I not dug in my heels, taken all their names, threatened to charge them with malpractice if he bled to death, and take up with the health minister and *Four Corners* the fact that they had a charter to provide emergency triage for public patients, we would have had to drive for another thirty minutes to Nambour Hospital for attention. As it was, Geoffrey was already dying a thousand deaths because of my extremely unattractive harridan behaviour. They relented, shot him full of tetanus vaccine, stitched up the gash and sent us home. It still makes my blood boil that medicine is for sale to the highest bidder and not given willingly to those whose need is most pressing, regardless of their bank account.

I'm not without my own health setbacks. I am an ageing female with a belly full of fibroids and cysts, hypertension, menopause, allergies, but mostly plumbing problems. None of it is so serious yet that I need to be burdening the already groaning health system with my troubles, but sooner or later, that cyst is gonna blow, possibly causing peritonitis, or the fibroids could go feral and get bigger instead of smaller as I get older. Without health insurance, all I've got to go on is hope and faith that if I end up in pain, someone will take pity on me and give me the drugs. If not, I guess there's always the option to sell up, acquire a heroin mountain and work through it till I attain Nirvana.

Bloody plumbing, it gets to the cows too. A lifetime of reproduction doesn't come without its cost. Poor Number Eighty calved about a month ago and prolapsed. With no prior gynaecological experience of cows whatsoever, I diagnosed that something was wrong, on account of the pendulous lotus bud of flesh hanging out of her rear end, but had no idea what this might be. I thought: *Maybe afterbirth?* But that usually separates when the calf drops and looks more like a long, straggly collection of gizzards. It wasn't till Joanna got home from work and had a closer look that we found out what it was. She rang the vet who suggested we try pushing it back in. She's at least done ag-science and a meat inspector's course with the Department of Primary Industries, and we were dealing with meat, I suppose. However, Number Eighty was most certainly alive, and I doubted she'd be keen on cooperating with a bunch of humans fiddling about with a bit of herself she couldn't see.

We led her into the crush and the three of us, Joanna, Geoffrey and I, started pushing, but not hard enough to counter *her* pushing back. Eventually we admitted defeat and called the vet, who arrived armed with an epidural, know-how and an excellent crush-side manner. He said the sweetest thing; made me feel less weird about my thoughts on the humanity of cows. 'Look, she looks really grateful, as if she's saying thank you.' I fell in love with him instantly. Perhaps he really did see the same look in her eye that I did; or maybe it was the look in my eye he'd seen, as I winced with every shove. And when he finally, gently, pushed her cervix back in and sutured her vulva, had he noticed me shiver at the cell memory of my own perineal stitches?

I took the stitch out of her myself a week or so later, with surprising ease. She didn't even seem to notice. Because the prescribed antibiotics had unfortunately sent her into decline while she fed her calf, we weaned it early to take the stress off her, but it never really got that vital start and is still runty. We'll have to sell her if she prolapses again — vet bills cost more than the price of a calf. Still, I am grateful that he made that house call just on dusk, got covered in gallons of urine, and was willing to treat her in the glow of his car headlights.

Though I love to see the newborns up close, I hope I never have to deliver a difficult birth. I have no desire to see my whole arm disappear into a cow's back door to try and work out what's wrong. I've heard horror stories about attaching chains to the little legs inside to pull the baby free with a tractor. Thankfully, our cows have so far managed to do the birth thing all by themselves. I've never seen an actual delivery, but I have encountered calves so new they are still wet and slippery in a puddle of waters.

It is an intimate intrusion, but the cows know me well enough now to make only a mild show of snorting protectiveness. Really, I think they know how profoundly impressed I am by their offspring, and like to show off. I get the feeling that they know that I know that they know I won't hurt their babies (well, not yet anyway), because the sight of these brand-new creatures generally reduces me to tears, and cows understand tears.

I know this because we lost Number Seventy-five a year ago. After she dropped her last calf I noticed her limping. It didn't look too out of the ordinary — they often limp a little until their hips slide back into place after the birth. But on closer inspection, I saw that she was suffering from an extremely tender, swollen foot. We let it go, hoping she'd get over it, but she began to lose weight and was obviously struggling to get down to the dam to drink, so we slowly guided her down to the yards and called the vet. He found an enormous infected abscess between her claws, drained and dressed it, and left us with ten daily doses of antibiotics to inject into her.

You get to know an animal when it's sick. She stayed in the yards with her calf for the duration and we took water and lucerne to her. On the last day we put her in the crush to take the dressing off and see how the wound was looking. *Phwaw*, the stink was dreadful and all the hair was gone from the skin under the bandage. It was difficult to do, and awkward, and she threatened to fall in the crush from exhaustion and pain, but I finally got it unbound and bathed and disinfected.

Geoffrey opened the side gate of the crush and she stumbled out into the yard, limping and shaking, and then I looked into her eyes. She was crying — tears streaming down her face — and I burst into tears, too. Her calf stared at me accusingly: *You are responsible!* And it was right. It was all my fault. I didn't react soon enough to her initial signs of distress — and as it turned out, she didn't recover. Her foot got worse and we had to make the awful decision to get her onto a truck before she went down in the paddock. I still feel like a heel for putting her through all that agony for nothing. I will never forget her tears.

So, since I seem to have become an amateur vet in my middle age, I can't see why I shouldn't aspire to amateur doctor as well. Seems everybody is doing it. There are hundreds of 'alternative health professionals' up here — chiropractors, massage therapists, acupuncturists, herbalists, Reiki masters, almost all as expensive as the mainstream medicos. 'Alternative health' isn't really alternative — what the medical profession means by that mildly derogatory term is *traditional* medicine. The old witches' brews aren't just old wives' tales — they worked for my grandmothers, and just because some multinational company can't work out how to synthesise a plant drug, and therefore discounts its efficacy, doesn't mean it doesn't work. Chinese and Ayurvedic medicine do, too. Even eighty-year-old Joe is devoted to the acupuncturist who provides relief for the sore feet that his doctor could never fix.

I am eternally grateful for the fact that I don't hobble around on built-up shoes like my, and my son's, polio-afflicted grandfathers did, and I'm kind of pleased that I didn't die in childbirth, which my grandmother's generation risked with every pregnancy, and yes, birth control is cool. But modern medicine is not terribly good at treating the ordinary infirmities of excess that I will no doubt suffer when it all finally catches up with me.

So I'm planning to grow my very own pharmacy — an alchemical garden — to make my own snake oil. Alchemists were the first scientists. Although most people associate alchemy with turning base metals into gold, in reality the majority of alchemists worked in 'spagyrics': the extraction of the curative compounds in plants. Paraceleus, perhaps the most famous, was primarily concerned with healing. My friend Therese attributes my current fascination with arcane knowledge to what she calls my Renaissance-woman complex. I can't quite work out whether this is a compliment or not: is she talking about my eternally optimistic view that if something is written down I feel perfectly capable of getting my head around it, or does it mean that I am a jack of all trades and master of none? Still, I've got a collection of medicinal plants and a library of books, herbals and pharmacopoeia, containing all the collected wisdom of the ages for the preparation of the tinctures, ointments, poultices and antiseptics that I'll need to treat myself, as the wheels fall off my generally robust health.

While most of the medications we rely on for pain relief, like opiates and aspirin, are derived from plants, their extraction and production should, of course, be kept out of the hands of amateurs like me. But there's eucalyptus oil for the chest, tea-tree oil for infections, pawpaw, calendula and aloe for skin ailments, valerian for insomnia. And let's not forget grapes for wine.

Food itself is medication against the pain of hunger; and, more often than not, it is only the application of either a little heat or time to a plant that releases its healing properties. An infusion taken as tea, a steaming wad on a wound, or a tincture, can be as effective as a fistful of pills. And best of all, I don't have to pay some US drug corporation for the fancy packaging.

I was much more comforted as a clogged-up, sniffling child by eucalyptus oil in petroleum jelly (that's all a vaporub is) lovingly rubbed onto my heaving chest, than by forcing down an unswallowable antibiotic. I recently found a remedy for tick bite that is based on the idea that you look for the cure near the cause. Bluetop, that common weed that bursts into lovely fluffy mauve blossom, works like an antihistamine. I collect its heads as soon as it flowers, douse them in vodka and let them stand in a jar. Applied to the tick bite, the alcohol cools the itch, while at the same time the bluetop takes out the swelling. The tincture resides in my medicine cabinet — cheap, extremely effective, and completely without any side effects.

How did we forget all this stuff in only a couple of generations? My grandmothers raised their children in the bush without scripts for antibiotics or invasive surgery. Sure, they had to endure dreadful epidemics of diphtheria, polio, measles, croup, chicken pox and flu — and many died from the serious ailments without the modern medicines we have available now — but the little things, ear infections, colds, fever and debility, they dealt with at home, cooking up remedies on the stove. My mother had her home remedies and used them to treat all my childhood ills. I hope to be up to speed with my own when it is my turn to care for her. There is no cure for old age, except death of course; the best to be hoped for is relief from the slow pain of it.

But for now I'm practising on the lower-order animals. My front verandah currently doubles as an infirmary which I guess will eventually grow into a full-on nursing home for the ageing Coven. Hen Linda is in decline. She is down with a paralysis that seems to afflict layers in their dotage, which for a chicken, pumping out an egg a day, is only about three years of age. However, she's not in pain, she just can't walk.

In the dome this meant she could no longer avoid the vindictive beak of Twenty, the neurotic bitch from hell, and couldn't get at her share of the food, couldn't scratch and couldn't get to the night-time perch. So now she leads a life of ease by the kitchen front door, where she reclines in a foam box, gorges herself on kitchen tidbits, and considers herself fully human, because I have become completely fond of her clucking, close proximity.

We converse, me in human, she in chicken, and we seem to understand each other. Who'd have thought — a talking chicken? I know when she wants a spin on the grass, and she has a particular excited cluck of gratitude if I shave fresh corn off the cob for her. Lately she's become the guard chook, and lets me know if any unwelcome creatures venture onto her patch. She does a fair bit of thinking in the meantime, evolving her consciousness to a higher plane, I imagine — or something.

Most of the Coven are approaching their last legs and, one after the other, they'll hit the retirement home on the verandah, where they will be renamed Sookachook and live out the remainder of their days in comfort. I can't bring myself to do them in — besides, who would eat an ailing animal? Once they have become Sookachook, they relinquish their Coven name and it is given to a newer, younger model. 'Hen Linda' is now a gleaming white, red-combed young pullet, a very attractive creature, while her predecessor, now Sookachook, enjoys her new exalted status.

I'm accustomed to the company of old chooks. There's been a procession of them through my life. Grandma, my paternal great-grandmother, lived till she was ninety-one. She wasn't just old, she was ancient; all crepe-jowled softness and white, fly-away hair. Her eyelids were heavy and I always thought she was only ever barely awake. But it was encroaching blindness that drew her shades down and, as it did, her domestic world dimmed too. Her house was always dark and mysterious when we visited as kids.

Out the back she kept a small vegetable garden and chooks which she culled and dressed each Christmas for her family. It was her festive gift — the only thing she had to trade for love and belonging, and even though I was still small, I understood that the meal made of Grandma's chicken was to be savoured for all the time and love invested in it. I don't remember ever having this pointed out to me — I think I just absorbed it. Dad adored his grandma and we followed suit.

There'd been a rift of some sort between her and her daughter-in-law — my dad's mum — which never healed, and it fell to her grandchildren to share the load of caring for her in her seemingly endless old age. Mum used to take us to visit her on weekends, when Grandma made us sandwiches from a huge bottle of Vegemite that must have been in her pantry for about a hundred and fifty years. It was hideously stale, but we ate those sammos whether we liked them or not, because she'd gone to the trouble to keep it there, for us. We were never allowed to be ungrateful.

I remember one visit vividly. While we were there a panicking elderly neighbour came to Grandma's front door because her husband wasn't breathing — and I heard my confident little thirteen-year-old voice pipe up, 'I know mouth to mouth.' I'd done a lifesaving course at school. But the plastic dummy with the removable mouthpiece hadn't prepared me for the reality — of removing the old man's teeth or pressing my lips to his wrinkled blue ones.

He smelt of aftershave and black tea, and though I managed somehow to resist my gag reflex for the full three minutes, he didn't recover. Hs skin was cold and grey and he'd probably been dead for a while before his wife managed to find help. But for several years without fail, on the anniversary of that dreadful day, I received a card from her in an increasingly crabbed hand, which struggled to find a way to thank me for my failed attempt to revive her old man.

Then soon after, it happened again. On holidays at the river, I was fooling around with my cousins down on the riverbank and suddenly there was a flurry of activity on the shore, our fathers pointing and shouting. We could just make out the bobbing bald head of a man floating face down in the shallows, as my uncle's boat cut a wake speeding towards him. Soon, the body was sprawled on the beach, shocking and white as a bloated toad fish — and again I was going through the motions: turn the body, clear the airways, pinch the nose, make a seal and blow. But all I got was a horrible farting sound — the air wouldn't go in! His lungs were not only full of water, but strands of long black weed. Afterwards, they said he'd had a heart attack and drowned, watched by mud crabs and tiddlers in the shallows of the weed beds.

So when it was my own grandfather's body I discovered one morning, grey-lipped and blue, I just let him be. I knew there was nothing for it. I knew the taste of death, and I knew the feeling of it — the emptiness — he'd already gone. He was only sixty-five. Grandma would outlive him for many years, but she never really got over losing her adored eldest son. I used to wonder how long it would be before we'd find her, lifeless in the still, lonely silence of her house.

Her final batch of chickens was a mess. She had dressed them and wrapped them in newspaper for distribution, but when we got them home and my mother opened hers, she found it bristling with quills and fuzz. Not only was Grandma's eyesight failing, but her sense of touch was retreating, too. They called it arthritis and, soon after, the decision had to be made to put her into a nursing home. She turned ninety-one the same year I turned nineteen, which at the time I thought bound us together in some strange numerologically mystical way, but I was really only bound to her in a much more commonplace way. Familiarity.

My dad has a drawing of her from the last year she was living in the home. It is in *conte* pastel, so I must have been at art school by then. Funny thing is, I don't actually remember doing it. I recall the day, the mild irritation of having to visit Grandma when I no doubt had something much more adolescently important to do, so I pretentiously took along a sketchpad to make a point about how bored I intended to be. Mum would always take a tin of Arnott's bickies, share a cup of tea with her, chat about family gossip, replace old underwear, replenish her stock of denture creme. She'd brush and re-plait Grandma's hair amid all those unmistakable but muffled hospital noises of bedpans, trundling tea trolleys and tinkling cutlery on thick, cheap china.

I must have decided to draw her, and she must have been looking directly at me, but I have no recollection of it till the moment she stared back at me from the page, this nonagenarian woman in all her power and splendid experience. I don't know how I did it, or where it came from. I do remember that for one scary moment I recognised myself looking back at me from a distant future.

Both of my grandmothers made it to the same lengthy age. The chicks in my family stick around. This is not necessarily a blessing, and the idea of reaching such a great age fills me with dismay. I'm halfway there, have amassed the princely sum of twelve thousand dollars in super, and have only one child. So far it's not looking good for a comfortable retirement in the manner in which I'd like it to pan out. Last time I looked, none of the scrap heaps they send paupers to die on advocates the red wine diet, nor even prescribes it for medicinal purposes! I'll just have to rely on karma in my dotage. I've watched my parents care for theirs and I've moved here where I can care for mine. They are still independent, but eventually my sisters and I will do the shopping and cooking and keep whoever lasts longer company. And I'll be doing it gladly. It's not so much a duty as an opportunity to set an example for my son.

I took him to visit my maternal grandmother before she finally fell off her perch. There was so much time and history transmitted in her last caress of his cheek — a caress that spanned generations of experience and wonder.

She had never flown in a plane, never seen a masterpiece in a gallery, she never saw a play. All they had in common was the family face that passed through hers into his.

The last Christmas before her bones turned to ashes inside her and she had to go to the home, I had the chance to talk with her, on the landing at my parents' house. We sat on the stair smoking my posh expensive brand, and I asked if she was afraid to die. She was as candid as my abrupt question required — 'No, I reckon I'll just go to sleep.' I don't know if she was only trying to soothe and protect me from having to confront my own mortality, or avoid it herself, but that's just what she did in the end: she went to sleep and didn't wake up. Pleasingly, though she smoked and drank, she died of a natural cause: longevity.

Caring for ageing parents isn't an easy option these days, especially if you've got a mortgage, need two incomes to support the kids who've popped out much later than last generation's, and will have to contemplate a third income to look after Nanna's aged care. It's a vicious circle: work three times the hours to pay for someone else to do what we are perfectly capable of doing for ourselves. Service industries.

Everyone, it seems, though mostly women, is engaged in service industries, and *they* have to pay other service providers to provide the same services to their own families that they provide to others. I guess it's a question of value. Women's work is finally adding up to its true cost. We're out in the work force getting paid to do the things we used to do for love. Something is getting wildly out of whack here, and I can't help but think it is incredibly wasteful and soul destroying. *But then, love isn't taxable income.*

Being employed and feeling needed are two entirely different things. To be needed by another person, and to make a contribution to their wellbeing, is not the same as being paid money for a service. Somehow, the mutuality of the exchange is diminished by money. Sure, I get paid to teach, but no one could afford to pay me for all the time and energy that goes into my concept of the social contract I have entered into.

Vocation. A calling. A mother responds to her baby because it calls and she hears. Likewise nurses, youth workers, legal aid lawyers, meals-on-wheels volunteers, firies, nuns, even the odd copper, all hear the voice of need and respond. There is a warm fuzziness about doing something for someone you love, and if your work involves the public, sooner or later it gets personal, and turns into something like love. The kids at school are all my children now, and I want the same things for them that I want for my own child. I have worked out what they need, and am doing my best to provide it for them.

*   *   *

Sookachook needs me and I love to be regarded by her beady little eye, her head cocked to one side, trying to work out what the hell I am, why my face is all puffy and my nose running and why I seem so heavy on my feet, and thinking to herself, *Oh no, human flu!* But she lets me pick her up and take her onto my lap and stroke her silken feathers. The verandah jasmine has burst into early bloom, and we swoon, wreathed in its potent sweet scent, strong enough to penetrate my stuffy head. As the orange light of the sunset behind us ignites the trunks of trees and highlights in fluorescent pink the passage of fleeing clouds, my most necessary human comes upstairs onto the verandah from his studio.

He's been down there for days and, as I seldom go into the studio unless I am working on something with him or we're playing music together, I've lost track of what he's up to. He leans over me from behind, kisses the crown of my head and places a CD on the table in front of me. I can just make out his handwriting on the case in the falling darkness:

For Her Birthday, 2006.

spring

6th September

Rainfall last month: only half an inch

Jobs for this month:

- Sow — 3rd & 4th: Balinese corn, herbs (rosemary, lemon balm), rosella test crop.
- Collect dry cow pats, sift for seedling mix.
- Compost into beds 5 & 6.
- Move chooks off the back garden, to front.
- Branding.
- Send calves to market.
- Prick out seedlings.
- Clean pump foot valve.
- Choir practice Monday afternoons.
- Workshop hospital scene, block acts 1 & 2.

Geoffrey's gift is on, again. I've been playing it non-stop and can understand completely why a queen would keep a court composer. His music is the lavish adornment to my interior life — a portable pleasure, an instantly accessible eddy of time in my imagination. I've listened to it so many times now that I feel every heartbeat and emotion caught up in its flow. It is our deepest conversation. I hear his music like a prayer.

There are four pieces on it, but the last one gets the most airplay on Radio-me, a song we worked on together. It begins with a cascading fanfare of trumpets, layered and spiralling round each other. A little motif rises out of it and the trumpets make way for a beating impetus that feels like impulsion through space. Then my own voice. It makes my whole body tingle with the strange sensation of being penetrated by myself, a hall of sound mirrors. He has transformed my voice into a choir of angels, racing each other through the void, singing up creation. My part of the song is about a little particle and wave of light so in love with each other that they leap-frog through the vacuum, not knowing where they are going, just round and round each other, and the energy they create propels their journey. Geoffrey's rich deep monotone pre-empts my melody with:

Come, leave the past behind you
Come, even dreams might bind you
Turn from all that blinds you
There in light I'll find you …

and it never fails to get me because I am a sentimental fool and I am deep in love, and you don't get a gift like that every day of the week.

Sookachook agrees, she sings along too. Something, some note or interval sets her off and she's not bad, occasionally out of time but never off-key. The rest of the local, earthly, winged chorus chimes in as well. Spring brings them all out for the mating season. Tiny red and grey finches no bigger than my little finger titter in the long dry grass, its rustling somehow amplifying their volume. And the Geoffrey bird is back, calling his name over and over, and the La Cucaracha birds who sing the first line of that old fifties melody in their haunting voices, piping through the valley in a round. And the green Howling-Baby bird (catbird, to people who have cats) is back looking for love in the trees behind my shade house. All their songs are mixed in with mine now, and in the evenings cicadas latch onto my top end. The only element missing is the Audience frogs, but they won't applaud till it rains.

I gave a gift of music to the kids last term. Their heads are filled with the music snaking in through the leads of their iPods. It is a constant soundtrack to their lives, but it's insular and personal, and they get almost no opportunity to hear or see live music and experience it as a group — an audience. They were pretty weirded out when I asked them to lie down with their heads in the centre of a circle, on the floor of the darkened music room. They had to be still, eyes closed and not distract anyone else for the duration of the music. Practically impossible for some. I had to patrol the interior like a bossy matron. But then the music took them over. It was a piece by a contemporary group called Hybrid, which I knew would have a hook for them — a good solid dance beat, but the work is overlayed with a classical feel — no lyrics, just music. It is a wonderful soaring piece and it got them. For an entire twenty minutes, after the giggles and nudges subsided, they let themselves just listen and concentrate on the space it filled inside them.

When it was over, they could not contain their pleasure. Beaming smiling faces flushed with the exhilaration of the experience, everyone talking at once to no one in particular about the journey they'd just been on. 'I felt like I was flying; planets were exploding', 'I was on my bike and sailing over a jump…', and my eyes teared up. Someone asked what was wrong. 'Nothing, everything is right. I love you guys', was all I could come up with.

Moments like this are rare and beautiful. To amaze them, to see their fire lit and the sparks of recognition arc between them. I could get used to this. It makes all the shouting and exasperation and the drudgery of marking and scoring worth it. This is what teaching is —

the chance to share the thing you love the most with young minds, to show them that it all happens inside your body and between your ears. To give them the opportunity to feel what perception can be, and how to live in a world of vibrant sensation. But best of all was showing them the physicality of their excitement.

We conducted an experiment afterwards. They took each other's pulses, observed skin colour, noted goose pimples. Some reported red rashes blooming on necks, others noticed prickly scalps and sweaty hands. Ten minutes later, we went through the symptoms again, when the heart rates had slowed and breathing had calmed. If you didn't know they'd just had a brush with beauty, you'd think they'd all come down with a fever. In a way they had. It was contagious.

I think that was the day I agreed to run a community choir after school. The idea was to get the school to be more 'community involved', to be able to tick the box for a funding grant or something, and I was value-added. Another hour in my day suddenly vanished, because in the delirium of my response to the kids' excitement, I said *yes, yes, yes.*

Ouch! There's a bright smear of blood in the palm of my hand. In the other is a scrubbing brush, and between my knees, a bucket of water. I appear to have been cleaning out the pump's foot valve, but I have no idea how long I've been squatting here, by the edge of the dam below the garden. The mozzie has brought me back to Earth. What if this one carries Ross River fever? I push the idea away as I wipe my blood off on my thigh and reach for the bite on my bum, already itchy.

I've been absorbed in watching the life of a Lilliputian city in a fallen log beside me. Hollow furrows have rotted out along its length, and there, in the shelter of their moist cover, gazillions of tiny creatures have made a home and are engaged in the serious business of existence. A skink flickers past, a fly, bottle-blue and green, helicopters above a nest of ants that has been displaced by a roach attack. They frantically drag egg cases, their next generation, to safety, avoiding webs stretched across the narrow alleys. But it's not only this drama that has me captivated.

I'm seeing it through the prism of a painting: *Journey into the You Beaut Country*, the first image I ever spent a long time looking at. I was sixteen, and the high-school art project for the week was to tonally render an existing work of art. We could choose any artist in the Queensland Art Gallery collection — I chose John Olsen. I thought it would be easy to reproduce the scribble of nonsense it seemed to be at first glance, but when I started to try to work it out, with eye-squinting focus on its complex detail, I was startled by how much information it contained. It took me days to decode that picture and transmute it into a representation of darkness and light. By going through that process, I'd etched that image into my mind.

The picture is alive, all ochres and energy, bursting with fluid virtuosic drawing. Olsen must have sat beside a similar log at the water's edge and peered into the world of its inhabitants. Have I noticed the log because knowing that painting has shown me what to look for, or am I recalling the painting because I am seeing it in the log? It's hard to know which perception has inspired the other, but now, with the living breathing subject superimposed on the artist's static representation of it in my mind, I get what Olsen was trying to do. It isn't a snapshot of the natural world, but rather, about its passage through time. What I mistook for tendrils and fronds are more like ant trails and lizard paths, or the zigzagging flight of a dragonfly. What I thought were mere doodles and dots now appears to be the trailing bubbles of a tadpole just beneath the surface of the water, or the spoogey passage of a caterpillar. Plants explode into life and die, simultaneously, flowers bloom and wither in the blink of an eye. Using only two dimensions, he has tried to bypass three, and paint the fourth dimension, time. Perhaps. I can't know any of this for sure — it is only an idea, but now I'm stung by it, I won't be able to stop scratching till I've figured it out.

September is the cruellest month up here, and it is with some trepidation that I set out today. It's been so cold and dry that the inside of my face feels scoured by a glacier. Then as soon as the season changes, the rise in temperature and a little more moisture in the air encourages the bugs, which have struggled to survive winter, to go forth and multiply.

'Tis the season for infection, and one of the most reliable places to pick one up is school. Maybe my cold last month will make me immune to the soup of disease that festers in the classroom. Primary school offers a wide range of ear, nose and throat infections. One kid comes to school with a virus and half a dozen shared coloured-pencil sucks later — pandemic.

Then there's infants. A zoo of wildlife spawns among them in the warmer weather. The horror of head lice.

There has been a bit of a fashion statement going round school lately. The cool guys began to turn up with number-one buzz cuts and beanies pulled down low to look like 'gangstas'. In my ignorance I've managed to ruin the whole pop-culture effect by adopting a worried brow and sympathising: 'Nits?' If I do get them, I'm seriously thinking of getting a number-one cut myself, and a beanie, which should finish off the look for good.

Scariest, though, is high school. I have to be doubly wary of them, because of their capacity to infect mental health, especially in spring — mating season. Almost overnight the Year 8s go completely stupid. Normally quiet, intelligent, careful children turn into raging monsters. Boys, previously lithe and energetic, are suddenly dragging their knuckles on the ground and losing control of their voices. The girls lose any understanding of the English language because, *like, they're really busy, like, inventing, like, their own*! I once passed notes under the desk that said dumb things like:

'He want's to go with you.'

Nowadays they're texting each other in SMS code, which they know I can't decipher if I confiscate the mobiles.

It takes all my concentration to remain aloof from their turmoil; it is highly infectious, especially since we've begun rehearsing the play. Its subject matter is pre-teen angst and desire for belonging and acceptance in the group, and the characters have to work through the fear and exhilaration of discovering who they are in relation to each other, which is precisely what my cast is in the process of doing in its own real life. Every emotional dummy-spit is magnified. They don't call it drama for nothing.

We've had tears, a threatened mass walk-out, a sacking, a kid leaving the school, recasting of two roles, two characters to cut from the script, and most still don't know their lines. They are angry at me for pushing them beyond what they think is their boundary, and can't understand the difference between teacher and director. I try to explain to them that what we are doing is creating a world, and that if we are going to create a world we need a creator, and in the beginning was the word, which is the script. So therefore I am God and they are subject to my will. But they don't get it, and fight like the devil against my self-proclaimed authority. But I forgive them, because they have no idea what they are doing. Yet.

Most of these kids have never been inside a theatre, never sat in a dark room and suspended their disbelief to watch people convincingly transform themselves into characters. A handful of Year 10s are my production crew, and so far stubbornly resist what I am asking them to do. They've read the play, but don't understand why they need to memorise it, seeing as they're not acting. I try to impress upon them that backstage is the same thing, that everyone involved is on show, except that they won't be seen. They are lethargic, almost impossible to motivate, and a little bit annoyed that I'm asking them to read books on the subject and write an assignment. Turns out performing arts isn't the loaf they had hoped for.

A few of the cast are into it, though they are still torn between their growing passion for the play and their need to belong to the larger group. The four key leads have rehearsed a couple of scenes and have a glimmer of an idea of how to imagine themselves into their roles. I'm desperately hoping that their energy will become intense enough to infect the others. There must be at least one receptor on this organism which the virus of comprehension can latch onto and mutate, but their immunity is pretty strong, and I'll have to supply an equal and opposite charge to their negativity till the contagion is complete. It takes every ounce of energy I've got — thank goodness it's only two days a week or I'd be a basket case by now. Unlike the God of Genesis, I don't have the option of expulsion, and besides, I want them to taste the fruit of my tree.

But knowledge is a two-way street, and these country kids have a wealth of information I need. They are a bit confused by the role-reversal of me asking them questions, but are quite chuffed to be able to teach me stuff they know. One of the boys has lived with cattle all his life and I'm curious about branding. Does it hurt? What's the best way to do it? Are there alternatives?

The main thing I want to know springs from something that we observed last week. It's the first time I've ever seen cattle branded, and the first time Geoffrey has ever done it. All the new cows entering the herd have to be done because ear tags can go missing occasionally, and if cattle push through a boundary fence, they can go for a bit of a wander. I just know Number One would be the kind of girl to develop a taste for shopping if she ever finds her way to town and discovers what it is.

We get the dozen or so cows into the race while the iron heats up in the coals of a fire built in the yards. It is a physical thing to do — the iron is heavy, and a cow's rump is about chest height, so Geoffrey has to hold it high above his head and lunge the red-hot brand down firmly and cleanly onto the hide, careful not to slip and smudge the impression. The air fills with the acrid stink of singed hair and burnt fat. Then we notice the most extraordinary thing. After the first couple of brandings, the cows lined up in the race start to lick the spot that is going to hurt. They can't see what is going on up ahead in the crush, and they've never seen it happen before, but somehow they all know that something hot is going to burn their bum, and precisely where it will land.

I put this to my young cattleman who simply says, 'They all do that.' I explain that they couldn't see it — 'How do they know?' 'They just do, Miss.' This seems a perfectly reasonable answer to him, even though I press on with, 'But *how* do they know?' He isn't prepared to elaborate, so I change the subject to our lesbian cows.

I've seen cows out in the paddock mounting each other and thought it was maybe a pecking-order thing — they have one: there is a boss cow and the position is doggedly defended, especially when new girls join the herd. My cowboy quite calmly informs me that they do this to show the bull which of them is coming into season. Apparently, the one on the bottom is on heat. I ask him why they need to do that. He looks at me as if I'm, *like, totally brain dead*: 'There's a lot of cows and only one bull, he can't be everywhere at once.'

I have to leave it at that because suddenly there is an alarm bell screaming and the kids are already lining up. They know the drill and, because they can't smell any smoke, know it's *only* a drill and they eagerly file out onto the oval, pleased by the disruption to classes. The little kids are delighted by the sight of the bushfire brigade guys (fathers of some of them) in their bright yellow, silver-reflector-piped overalls and shiny helmets. After the lecture on fire safety and the need for them all to stay calm, stay put and get their names crossed off the roll, the infants will get a guided tour of the big shiny water trucks parked on the oval.

It's going to take all afternoon to hose them down and get their minds back onto school work after such a big adventure. I've got them for drama, so instead of even trying to change the subject, we do firefighting role-plays rather than the lessons I had planned. Year 2 prove to be very accomplished little mime artists, passing imaginary buckets, unrolling hoses and reacting to the sudden pressure when I pretend to turn on the water.

The last bell of the day rings just before my energy ebbs away entirely, leaving me only fifteen minutes to guzzle a coffee and collect myself before the choir arrives for practice. We are rehearsing outside because their first gig, already booked, is to perform outdoors at the local show. I've taught them a little gospel rock'n'roll number with a couple of harmony parts, and today, out under the trees, they give it up. It sounds extraordinary and they all feel it, that moment when you sense yourself melt into the other voices and become part of a much bigger noise than you could ever make alone. They are all amateurs, people who didn't think they could sing, but boy, can they sing now! And the only thing I had to do with it was to peel away their self-consciousness. Too easy.

I listen to the taped performance all the way home, singing along, as pleased as a person has a right to be, but when I turn into our road at dusk, thick plumes of smoke are billowing up from our valley, purpling the setting sun, and my stomach leaps into a pit of fear. Fire! Shit! Where? Our place?

I'm fully expecting to be stampeded by our cows — but at the corner rounding the bottom of the hill where the road turns into a dirt lane, I relax a little. A neighbour who has been clearing his hillside for weeks has set fire to great piles of bulldozed timber and rubbish. Flames leap from three gigantic pyres three storeys into the air. One down by the road licks a stand of trees — these grow all the way along the dry gully that winds its way down through our valley. I gun the Valiant to get home before the conflagration I'm imagining reaches the jacaranda beside our house, mentally going through the stuff I can't bear to lose and where to stash it. Angry as a hornet, I wonder how anyone could be so stupid as to burn off in this weather.

But at home, I'm chastened by what's happened at our end of the valley while I was at school. Geoffrey has been rebuilding the pump house by the second dam, which shelters an old relic that still works after fifty years, having been lovingly cared for by his father. The blady grass here is a bit of a pest — the cattle won't eat it, so it grows high and papery-dry. Geoffrey was up a ladder today, grinding off a stubborn bolt that wouldn't undo, when a red-hot head ignited the grass below, and before he realised it the whole patch leading down to the water's edge was ablaze. He leaped from the ladder on a wave of adrenalin — *Use the pump? How?* And our cheap plastic bucket broke the moment he tried to use it to carry water from the dam.

By then the fire was heading for the ute parked up on the road above. Geoffrey sprinted round the edge of the spreading flames to drive it to safety, calling out to his father who was in the house further up the hill. Joe's a bit deaf and couldn't actually hear Geoffrey, but had by now smelt the smoke and come out onto the verandah to investigate.

Between them they put it out. Only a small grassfire, but it is still sobering to know how quickly one thing can lead to another. So easy to start — so hard to fix.

Neither fire got out of control but could have. We've often discussed ways to defend the house against fire. Our big, square iron roof would provide protection from falling embers. Our plan is to plug up the gutters and fill them with water. Anything valuable goes down into the studio under the house, which is to be lined with fireproof material. When the electricity goes down and the water pump fails, we'll need to dip into the tank by the house and resort to hand-pumping from portable backpacks to douse any spot fires that might start.

The whole valley is tinder dry after so little rain last month and desiccating westerly winds. We are desperate for rain, and though there's been the promise of it from the west, there's been nothing here. It is infuriating to hear of a storm in the next valley and not a drop falls in ours, or to see dark clouds looming only for them to pass behind the ridge. The dams are getting so low the waterlilies lie stranded and dying on their muddy edges. I've been pumping water to the garden twice a week, and my plants are starting to sag and wilt from the stress of coping with the pathogens that breed in still water. Rainwater contains something vital to their health, some mysterious property that makes them thrive, and they are panting for lack of whatever it is.

We occasionally visit friends who have built on a bush block. Their house is perched high on a ridge; a beautiful, simple space with a verandah jutting out into treetops on one side, and looking out over a spectacular view of their valley on the other. One afternoon when we were there, a storm swept through with rain so dense it turned the valley white, and as it approached the house, the edge of the squall fell like a curtain over the vista and hit like a truck, thrumming on corrugated iron at first, rising to a thunderous pounding roar at its most intense. Its impressive frenzy passed quickly, leaving the forest dripping, and the trunks of some of the eucalypts frothing, as if the water had been turned off while they were in the middle of washing their hair. A king parrot arrived at a feeder on the verandah, twice as vibrant for the darkened wet landscape behind him.

But I can't help thinking how it would be if that curtain was a cloud of smoke, rising from the earth; a fire flued up by the ridge, sucking plumes of oxygen into itself in its fearsome hunger, devouring everything in its path, its exhaust turning the valley black with ash. How would our friends manage to escape a wildfire? The drive from their place plunges down into a deep gully before it climbs up to the main road. Call me old-fashioned, or paranoid, but I prefer a buffer zone of at least a fallen tree width between me and the forest, and am quite happy to make the walk up the hill to take in a view, rather than risk living at the top of a forested ridge.

Eyes sparkling with excitement still, after twenty years, Joe tells a story about a bushfire that raced up the western side of the ridge bordering our farm: men with wet sugar bags and a water truck — himself gasping for breath as the fire crested the ridge — their panic and flight down into the valley. And he'll probably tell it again tonight over dinner, in light of the day's excitement.

Geoffrey has made shepherd's pie and invited his family down to our place. It's still cold at night so the fire is flickering behind its glass door. I've picked the last of the sugar snaps and broccoli, and even made pudding. Six-year-old Christopher and his mother Joanna will walk up the hill from their place, and Aunty Dizzy (as Christopher calls Geoffrey's other sister, Liz) will be here, too.

I have begun laying my dark pine table, and leave the finishing touches for Christopher, who loves the responsibility of setting out the silvery clinking cutlery right where it is supposed to go beside the plates. He's allowed to light the candles in two big chunky green-glazed curly-based holders that are too heavy for him to lift. They grow like plants out of umber rich darkness of the tabletop, and between them a large, clear glass bowl of nasturtiums erupts, red and orange and carmine yellow, hovering amid their circular bright green leaves.

Christopher loves to watch the candlelight reflected in the wineglasses and the way it makes everything glow. And he, like me, knows that Grandma likes napkins on the table, and he knows where to find them, folded stiff as cardboard, in the drawer under the lip of the table itself. Liz calls me a crawler for pandering to her mother's insistence on olde-worlde decorum, but really, I'm with Helen. I love starched linen and fine detail. Up-market restaurants charge a fortune for the pleasure of it — why not go there for free? It takes no extra effort. I have only one set of china — my best. And although it is all mismatched bits and pieces I've found second-hand, it is all white. An appropriate blank canvas for the food it will frame.

Till they arrive there's time for the cocktail hour. I'm being treated to a Geoffrey speciality. Cherry tomatoes are practically weeds round here and prone to promiscuity. They'll eventually crossbreed with any other variety I plant, and self-seed prolifically. One of the front beds has spontaneously erupted into a tangled patch of these spring sun traps. Every day for the past week the vines have produced a bowlful for Geoffrey to squish up to make tomato juice for his own invention: Cherry Mary — just add vodka.

While he makes the drinks I take a moment to feed the Minipecks, who are eating out of my hand now. It's a chance to see them up close. Their heads are small in proportion to their bulky bodies, which taper to an elongated tail. They step daintily on slender red feet with black fishnet-stockinged legs. Occasionally, they'll stand upright, chests and bellies thrust forward and wings held behind their backs, resembling pompous school masters. They come in two colours — pearl with pale grey, white-spotted feathers, and grey with charcoal feathers spotted white. In both, the feathers of their necks and backs are tinged with copper. The dominant male is always immaculate — never a feather out of place in his dark fledge. He spends a lot of time keeping the other two pearl males in order, by charging them, head down, wings folded but held up off his body like two fins. He's a coward when it comes to eating from my hand. The others can all overcome their fear, but he won't. Pride, I guess — can't bring himself to look dependent in any way.

Up this close, guinea fowl are extraordinarily beautiful for creatures that look as if their heads have been dipped into acid. Their throats are an intense violet blue, their red-rimmed wattles spring from the snow-white wrinkled, featherless flesh of their heads, and they have black markings above their eyes that make them look like they've all had facelifts, leaving them with perpetual individual expressions. The big guy looks stern; the pearl brothers, one confused, the other perplexed; and the females, a pearl and a grey, look anxious and fed up respectively. The total effect is topped off by a noble bony helmet, like a cassowary's.

Then there's Poofypeck, who doesn't know if it's Arthur or Martha — well, *it* may, but I don't: it's got one long floppy male wattle on one side of its beak, and on the other a petite feminine one, and it wears an expression of disbelief at its misfortune in being the outsider. I don't think the Minipecks are sure either, they all spend a lot of time charging at it, so this one's my favourite. Someone's got to love it.

The Minis are after-school therapy. As I watch them feed I consider my day, and try to place its events into the larger scheme of things. But sometimes none of it seems to add up to anything in particular. Mostly, life just goes on and takes its own time to filter down into meaning. Some stuff just sits out there on the edges of experience as little lumpy nuggets to keep in my pocket, to be felt and rubbed between fingertips.

Earlier this afternoon, after the fire drill, I had a spare moment to make a coffee and work out where I had got to with the rehearsals. On my way back from the staffroom, I came across a little boy who was waiting to see the visiting dentist. There he sat, afraid and alone on the step outside the scary dental van, with all its dreadful noises inside. When this boy first came to the school he only growled. He preferred to hide in corners and took no part in the larger activities of the group. But he liked music — perhaps it soothed the savage beast inside his nebulous little soul.

I went and sat beside him on the step. The sky was as heavy and ominous as the little black cloud of terror that had formed above his head. 'Smell that?' He looked up at me with big brimming eyes. 'Smell that black cloud? Smell the leaves up there sweating, and that still feeling on your skin?' He couldn't even grunt he was so frightened. 'That's the smell of rain coming.'

A moment later two enormous drops plopped on the asphalt at his feet, and another, chill as winter, split on his scabby knee and then his nose, and his face broke open in amazement at the witch who had magically produced the sunshower. His smile revealed a row of brown baby teeth, decayed down to little short stubs, but he looked like a boy who had just discovered a secret wonder of the universe, which, of course, he had. And we both sat there as the cloud above us burst into a promise of spring rains and the oily blue smell of wet bitumen steamed up. He was so delighted that I resisted my fear and loathing of the wildlife that was bound to be lurking in his dusty brush of brown hair, put my arm around his little shoulders and felt the last of his fear subside.

But I don't have time to figure my day out any longer. Christopher has arrived, the golden-glowing, bright, articulate creature. He's bathed in the light of his family's adoration, centre of all fond attention and fawning love, blissfully unaware of his mother's warning to the rest of us:

'Don't get too close, nits.'

7th October

Rainfall last month: Woo hoo! Four and a half inches!

Jobs for this month:

- Sow — 4th–6th: Aunty Ruby's Green tomatoes, Jimmy Nardello capsicum, Rosa Bianca aubergine. 13th: Golden beetroot, Dragon carrots, leeks. 23rd & 24th: broccoli, basil, Couve Tronchuda cabbage, celery, Great Lakes lettuce, parsley, Ruby Red chard.
- Plant out citrus.
- Harvest caulis, broad beans, turnips, replace with potatoes.
- Move chooks to front garden. Take this garden slowly. Dirt is full of gravel, barely any topsoil — needs a lot of conditioning.
- Cut tall stakes for snow peas. (Who would have thought they could grow so tall? Eight feet!)
- Play rehearsals — panic now!

The Coven has moved cross-country to the front garden beds again. In the process of carrying them over to the new position, I noticed that some of their toes had grown large, hard lumps. In some cases, the claws were completely embedded in these hideous growths, and the girls were finding it difficult to scratch. I'd never seen such a thing — not that I have much experience of chicken's feet outside of yum cha restaurants in Chinatown. Time to consult my trusty *Complete Book of Raising Livestock and Poultry*, but there's no mention of anything like it in there, either. After a week of asking around without becoming any wiser, I've decided to have a closer look. Hen Rachel is on my knee wrapped in a towel with her tooter in a bowl of soapy water as I try to clean it up enough to work out what is wrong.

As it turns out, it's just dirt. Last month's welcome late rainfalls turned the mulch in their dome to slush, the fibres wound round their claws and, matted together by wet clay, have since dried into hard reinforced balls. These are extremely difficult to dislodge, and need to be soaked to soften the clay enough to prise it away without hurting the bird's delicate pads.

So, here we are at Hughesy's *House of Beautay*, as one by one the Coven take turns at getting their nails done. They just love it, clucking like gossips at a hen's party, lapping up the attention and enjoying the eventual relief of getting that horrible hard thing off their toes. I use the opportunity to clip any ragged nail edges and check them for parasites. Because they move every two weeks and roost off the ground, they are louse- and worm-free. This weird toenail thing is the only problem they've ever had.

I've been indulging in a bit of personal maintenance myself lately, as well. I've had my batteries on recharge for the past two weeks — school holidays, and they didn't come a moment too soon. Three weeks of rehearsals with the kids during September nearly killed us all — well, I got close to nearly killing some of them. They have this two-week break to learn their lines and anyone who doesn't have them down word perfect when we go back to school next week knows he or she is going to die a slow, painful death.

There are only three rehearsals left before the play goes on, and we have to 'bump' into the beautiful big old wooden hall across the road from school. This involves transferring all the props, sets and their blocking onto the actual stage. The wings are tiny, and the stage itself acts like a gigantic speaker box, so every whisper and giggle can be heard perfectly, way down the back of the hall. Next week is our first full run-through, the week after we'll have the full technical rehearsal with the professional lighting guy, then the following week is full dress, and that's it.

Before the holidays I had to dress them down for their lack of concentration, slack approach to their rehearsals and general appalling behaviour towards each other. I told them that I no longer care about their play if they don't, and that seeing as my parents aren't coming to watch, I couldn't care less if they make a fool of me, but that they are going to look pretty stupid standing there, floundering and gaping like fish because they don't know their lines, or where to stand, or what to do next. *So there!*

I flounced out of the room to let them stew in their own juices. It was a pretty good performance, if I do say so myself: steam coming out of my ears, red face, pulling out of hair, verge of tears, hysteria. Worked a treat. Trouble is, I wasn't acting; it's personal now.

Before the end of the day several of the cast came to my room to apologise and promise that they'd do their best. Still, the only one off the hook is my leading lady. She has a huge part and is on stage for most of the play. She is quite rightly terrified, and secretly I'm astonished at her capacity to learn what she has already, but I don't let on. I tell her that as long as she knows exactly who her character is if the actual lines don't come, something close will, because she'll know what her character would say in the situation. Or even better, because she's got such big expressive eyes, she can use them to convey the emotion of what the line says. 'That will work just as well. Just don't panic.'

What a brilliant actor I am. I managed to give her all this calm, worldly wisdom as if I wasn't speaking from inside an emotional concrete mixer. I pushed my own panic button weeks ago, and had to somehow get it through their skulls that now is the make-or-break moment. I've already spent the entire performing arts budget for the year just getting the lighting organised. Everything else has to be done by hand, or by begging and borrowing. I still don't know if I've got backdrops, or where the hospital-set furniture is coming from. They've hardly collected any of the props they need, and Miss Hair-and-Make-Up-Department has gone feral and won't speak to me because she reckons I called her a bitch, when what I said was that she was behaving like one — two entirely different statements. *Dramarama.*

I still have six full days in which to grub around in my garden, muddy from a couple of good solid drops of an inch at a time. Nanna used to say, 'That was a good drop of rain,' and now I get what she meant. It really does drop, in huge painful bullets of gravity-driven wet. If you stay out in it, you come in with red, stinging skin from its lashing. We were down in Brisbane for one of them.

Geoffrey was involved in a fringe event at the Brisbane Writers Festival, one of a group of poets who were positioned around the site to commit random acts of poetry on an unsuspecting general public. Just at the moment they were scheduled to start, a black cloud swept up behind the city, across the river. Brisbane's prismic buildings suddenly crystallised before a great leaden front, and then it let go. We huddled under an open-sided shed as freezing horizontal rain sheeted in at us. It cleared quickly but we were drenched, and headed back to the Buddha's temple to dry off.

Therese was with us — we were staying at her place for the weekend. Therese is one of the artists who shared our floor of the warehouse in Sydney. She's about ten years younger than us, and has remained a firm friend. She moved from Sydney about the same time we did, and comes up to visit from Brisbane for a mental health break every so often. Because of Therese we'd arranged to see the painter Margaret Olley, in conversation at the festival.

From way up the back of the theatre, we could just see Margaret's diminutive figure curled into a too-large chair on stage, flanked by her biographer and her dealer. She looked like any little old lady, until she spoke. Mesmerising. I'd always discounted her as a flower painter, a maker of decorative still lifes to hang in middle-class living rooms and set off the drapery, but I am wrong. Regardless of my narrow taste, I now understand that she is the real thing. I see the example of the dogged, determined, single-minded life she has led. She chose to be a painter, made the sacrifices and has prevailed, with an enormous body of work to show for it.

Margaret Olley is my mother's age, but in our experiences she and I could be sisters: we grew up as children in the same green places, breathed the same humid air, felt the stifling repression of suburban Brisbane, and, at the same tender teen age, developed a burning desire to be artists.

I turned to see Therese, leaning forward, in thrall to the girls'-own story. She glanced at me, with great trembling tears welled up on her lower lids, and mine already wetting my cheeks. Afterwards we called it *our Margaret moment.*

There are more female painters a generation later, but the sacrifices are still the same. It takes a lot of pig-headed orneriness to insist on a room of one's own, and the time required to stick at the task. Therese is doing the hard yards, and still battles with the loneliness. It's not easy maintaining a relationship under those self-imposed conditions. And I wonder — had I stuck it out and made those demands on myself and the world, would I have had my son? Would I have found Geoffrey? Would I have ever left Brisbane?

I was an adolescent there during the Bjelke-Petersen regime of strong-arm tactics perpetrated against student activists in the seventies. It may be a vibrant modern city now, and has almost forgotten the planted drugs, the detention of young nay-sayers under the Health Act, when the cops arrived to raid our parties with their dogs, and their badges off. Modern Brisbane has repressed memories of the violence and rapes and backyard abortions and louts and smug conservative chauvanism. But I haven't. And no amount of renovation can completely conceal those deep cracks behind the city's swish new facade.

We were away from the farm for only one weekend but, emotionally, it felt longer — a journey into the past of the art world, the literary world, of Brisbane and the bad blood it causes to boil in me. So it was a relief to get back to my animals and chores, where I can switch the world off and just be. Besides, there is much to do in the garden. It is time to sow corn for the Coven, and now that I am flush with extra cash from teaching, I've purchased a small citrus grove that needs to be planted out in one row, on a cleared strip along the high side of the house above the driveway. West Indian lime and blood orange close to the kitchen for cocktail hour ease, mandarin, lemon Villa Franca, lemonade and a Washington navel.

Till they are bearing, I'll continue to walk up to the container paddock to collect oranges from the thirty-year-old tree that grows above the second dam. It sprang from Geoffrey's compost heap when he grew a garden there in his youth, and prolifically bears two crops of delicious sweet fruit every year, without fail. It is shorn from below at steer tongue height, and this year we pruned its upper branches for the first time in its life. It was too tall to harvest, so we took the middle out of its crown and can now climb up into it without being shredded by the spikes.

I also lashed out on a couple of big bales of mulch hay at the markets, and these will be delivered today. They have town markets up here, usually on Saturdays, and the mulch man drives his trailer up with a couple of bales on board and takes orders. It's a few days since I parted with the cash, and I'm just wondering if he's actually going to show up when I hear a truck coming. He turns into the driveway and leans out of the cab, asking me where I want it. The bales are twice as big as I remember them.

As we unload I decide I like him because he pays my pretty Minipecks a compliment — he likes guinea fowl, and wonders if I've got any fertilised eggs. He's got a clucky bantam and wouldn't mind hatching some. It just so happens that we discovered a nest in the long grass yesterday — there are four eggs there and he can have them if he wants. They won't last much longer before becoming dinner for the lace monitor anyway. Mulch man drives off pleased, leaving my two vast rolled mats of hay.

It takes me most of the day to pull them apart and spread the tree site with about eight inches of cover. Six holes, two foot deep and wide, six barrows of black, spongy rotted compost, and six hours later they are in.

And I am in the house of pain.

I think I might have overdone it. I manage to stay upright, make it inside and take to the mattress with my new best friend. Painkiller *forte*. Bugger traditional medicine. I can plant the corn tomorrow.

And tomorrow and tomorrow. Three days, it takes, to get back up again. I obviously don't know my own strength, which in light of this episode, appears to be piss-weak.

I've found muscles that were never in *Gray's Anatomy*, and all of them are stiff and sore, but I need to move, so I'm going for a walk to visit the cows. Geoffrey wants to do a headcount and open the top gate, but I'm not up to mountain climbing just yet. I'll hang out on the flat, down by the dam with Christopher, who has decided to come, too.

The herd has been in the big dam paddock for a couple of weeks now and have mowed it down to a smooth uniform lawn, dotted with their big black pats. They've cleared the long grass under the trees along the gully track edge — and there, white and stark, is a pile of loose bones. Ribs, two mandibles, half a pelvis and two scapulars, a fibula and other odd broken bits and pieces. Christopher is intrigued when we start assembling the bones into the imaginary creature that could be composed of this odd collection. We settle on a dragon dinosaur. It looks convincing enough to fool Darwin, and we decide to leave it there in case any passing palaeontologists fly over in a helicopter. Once Christopher has his tongue around it, he keeps rolling that delicious big word round and round his mouth like a lolly till it comes out right: 'Pay-lee-en-tol-o-gist.'

It is a beautiful day for a walk, so we take the rainforest alley to the cattle yards, cut across the middle dam wall and head up to the macadamia grove, planted at the top of the eastern ridge by a previous owner. There are a million things to stop and look at and discuss on the way; turtle heads popping up out of the muddy dam, a water monitor leaping off a fallen tree, huge yellow spider webs stretching across our path, and Panda's black calf lurking in the bushes, watching us.

But then, up on the eastern track, we pass through a

miasma of the unmistakable stink of death. Even Christopher knows it: 'Something's carked it.' We follow our noses to the corpse, thinking maybe a bird. *Hope it's the feral cat.*

We never dreamed it might be one of the cows. She's fallen from a steep verge on the other side of the gully. Maybe she slipped and lost her footing, or, nosing in among the lantana, didn't realise she was near the edge, and fell. Whatever, she hit the ground head first and broke her neck. She's black and swollen and looks ready to burst. It would explain all the commotion from the herd. She had a calf on her, and it had no choice but to wean itself. Geoffrey feels guilty and beats himself up that he didn't do a headcount when he shut the gate on that paddock, but there's nothing he could have done. Even if he'd discovered one was missing, she'd still have been dead.

A couple of days later, Grandpa comes back from one of his walks trailing a plume of ex-cow from his clothes. He's been up poking at her carcass to try to find her ear tag, so she can be crossed off in the ledger. He must have continued round to where the herd was grazing, to see what kind of condition the little orphan was in, and there encountered Christopher's dragon. Scratching his head, he asked if any of us knew anything about the bones of a strange creature he'd found in the paddock.

Christopher could barely contain his glee and nearly gave the game away.

In a couple of weeks the dead cow will be a pile of broken bits and pieces bleaching in the sun. It's amazing how quickly a body can disappear, out in the elements. She will fly apart in a slow-motion explosion. Her centre will not hold, her matter will disintegrate, her hide will turn to a powdery mat over her bones, and they will be dragged away one by one by scavengers. She'll be all but gone.

All the passion, all the tears and planning and intensity of our play will lead to one brief, ephemeral expression, and it will be over, all but gone. We're in the final stretch of the production now and I've spent most of the day shopping for last-minute props, some good-quality eye-liner and pancake — not easy to find in this neck of the woods — and still have to go over the script one last time, checking for anything I can cut at the end of the play if I have to. Four weeks till opening night and only three rehearsals left, two of which need to be done after dark to test the lighting — there are no black-out curtains in the hall — and I've a terrible feeling of foreboding in my bones that nothing will be ready in time.

We've bumped into the hall. This is the first chance to rehearse on stage with all the sets and props in place, and we're in the moment. They are up there, flying on nervous energy, actually doing it. I can't believe it. It's going to be okay. They almost have a full set of bones on which to flesh their characters. The leads have their lines down, they're remembering cues, and the Year 10s have finally realised what I mean by stage management. Although the curtain still seems to have a mind of its own, they've pretty much got the hang of it and are secretly glad we went to the trouble of setting out a cue sheet. I have delegated them to run the backstage so I can watch from front of house, where I furiously take notes and make last-minute amendments to the script.

They run out of steam about two-thirds of the way through because we haven't actually rehearsed the last part of the play in class, but now they know what they need to do, they are all focus and attention. It is really difficult to shout 'Be quiet backstage,' because I am now completely in love with everyone, and know it will all be all right on the night.

Geoffrey can't shut me up when I get home, still high, raving about how brilliant they are and how far they have come with so little actual time to work together to shape it into a living, breathing reality. While it's still fresh in my mind, I sit down to write up my notes. Rather than write them to myself, I decide to write a personal letter to each kid about their performance, what they need to do to improve it, things to watch out for, things to remember and generally fawn with enthusiasm, approval and excitement about how good the play is going to be because of their part in making it happen.

The following week in class, I hand them their letters before the evening technical rehearsal, and give them time to digest what I've written. We get down to set-change drills, run through the unrehearsed scenes, and set up a lunchtime rehearsal schedule for the days when I'm not there. I explain to them what will happen in the technical rehearsal and what I expect of them.

We are staying back after school and I'm feeding them; a sausage sizzle. They ignore my advice to drink water and get stuck into orange cordial. Half an hour later, one thing leads to another and they're spinning out — overexcited to be out after dark, albeit just across the road from school, and skittish as a yard of yearling fillies.

This is our only chance to test the stage make-up and it's not going well. Miss Hair-and-Make-Up spits the dummy when she realises that it's not a fashion parade, that stage make-up is difficult to master and requires her to think and concentrate on doing it my way instead of hers, and so she's off, hellbent on distracting everyone else in order to get up my nose. Her evil plan is working. She's halfway through the cast, with one in tears, my three leads hysterical and even the Year 10s losing patience with the ratty behaviour.

Just before it all turns nasty the daylight fades, and everyone noisily takes their places behind the curtain. I've warned them that stage lights are hot and that they have to conserve their energy, which, in the state they are in, has gone in one ear and out the other without passing through any grey matter at all.

And we're in the moment again, where time stands still and I feel like a midwife attending to the process of a difficult birth. The head is engaged, everything is going to plan, but I'm still anxious, checking all the vital signs, monitoring the pulse, timing contractions and managing the pain. And it is painful, but I think we're going to have a live baby. It may not emerge with all its fingers and toes, but its heart is definitely beating.

And there is a good omen — another birth on the horizon in my very own backyard. Poofypeck has been missing on and off for about a week, but now it doesn't come down to feed with the others or roost with them at night. I can hear it calling to them from the direction of the tree paddock and we've been searching up on the high dam wall, with no joy. But today, Geoffrey has found it. Thankfully, he noticed the gunmetal grey mass of Poofypeck near perfectly camouflaged by the dappled light from above, when he mowed only inches from its hiding place, tunnelled in under a screen of long grass. *She* is Mrs Mini now, sitting on a nest of forty eggs! Perhaps she wasn't afraid because she is familiar with the mower's roar.

The Minipecks derive enormous pleasure from the mower. They get excited as soon as it fires up and run from far corners of the garden to play chicken with it. It seems to be a guy thing — the females prefer to pick up the small creatures stirred up by the blades, but the males, who do not live by lizards, crickets and worms alone, dramatically charge each other for the right to fight the mower. No one ever wins, but there is little in life quite as amusing as watching Geoffrey's possessed ritual of mowing the lawn, surrounded by a tacking fleet of Minipecks. There he goes, St Francis of a Lawn Mower, man against the elements. As soon as it has rained, he's out in the wet grass mowing it down, so it doesn't get any ideas about getting out of control, with Minipecks in attendance in case the lawn mower gets any ideas about getting out of it without a fight.

I know Mrs Mini is in danger, nesting down on the ground. Once they go broody nothing will get them off the nest. I hope that because it's so close to the house, maybe the feral cat will stay away. We put an arch of curved tank-tin over her to keep her dry, put food and water down nearby, and keep our fingers crossed.

Over dinner and one or two glasses of red over the limit (but hey, no one's driving anywhere), we start to count our chickens. Geoffrey has contrived a fantasy poultry company and has already done an exponential tally of how many free-ranging Minipecks the valley could support, and how long it would take to fill the place. I think he got up to 370,000, but I suspect he's left out of the egg-laying equation that half of each generation would be male. By the time we got to that number, because they'd all be related to the original six brothers and sisters, we could have a fairly disgusting mutant breed on our hands. But he's undeterred and begins work on the sum again.

They are known as 'Tudor Turkey' when dressed and roasted. I giggle at the idea of self-beheading poultry, suggested by the name. We come up with brand names like *Henry's Consort*, or *Lady Di's*, and marketing campaigns that involve photoshoots with Therese in period dress, holding the hapless creatures in front of her rather generous bosom; we can't wait for her impending visit so we can inform her of her future fame. Whenever she arrives I get overexcited at the prospect of conversation with a like mind. We drink gallons of champagne on the first night, talk about art and life, become hilariously and ridiculously drunk and then she gets hay fever, raids my library, and spends the rest of the time in bed reading.

And true to our endlessly rehearsed script, this happens again, but today she is prepared and comes armed with all the gifts of modern medicine necessary to stave off her allergic reaction to the country. She has the energy to be doing my hair. Having taken pity on my extreme lack of girl skills, she has mixed three pots of colour to streak my grey to blonde, brown and purple. 'You can't be the director of a play and turn up to opening night looking plain,' she convinces me. Like the Coven, I find myself draped in a towel in the *House of Beautay*, getting the full treatment.

Therese is a sun shower, gone almost as soon as she arrives, leaving everything in her wake fresh, sparkling and green. Fuelled by her eager enthusiasm I feel I can face the last leg, our final dress rehearsal, and then there's nothing more I can do. The kids are on their own.

I hope the muses are up to the challenge, because we're going to need all the help we can get. Now is the time for me to stand back and let them work out their own problems. If I spoon-feed them through these final stages they won't learn anything from the experience and that is, after all, the point.

It's going to take every molecule of my resolve to

resist the temptation, though; I'm as sucked into the process as they are now and am finding it just as difficult to split hairs between the role of teacher and director as they do.

Last month I accepted a day supplying to one of the dead-posh private schools down on the coast. I swung the Valiant into the manicured grounds, made my way through a maze of brand-new, pristine buildings to the office and got my timetable for the day — art, music and supervision of a national science exam. The exam was first up. No sweat. Then art, in a purpose-built studio with shelves groaning with supplies — paper, paints, drawing materials, a library of books and posters, kiln, sculpture garden. You name it, they have it, in bulk. Then music. State-of-the-art studio computer technology, soundproofing, recording facilities, with no expense spared. Then I saw their theatre and rehearsal rooms crawling with black-clad serous young insects, workshopping scenes from Shakespeare, and felt my scalp prickle.

By 3.30 pm the chip on my shoulder had become so heavy, I could feel my feet dragging across the gravel of the car park. All these toys for the children of the well-to-do, and my little thespians have to struggle on nothing but a wing and a prayer. I wanted to cry for the sheer waste and selfishness. Imagine what could be achieved with all that privilege, all those materials and facilities. Imagine teaching kids who already play an instrument and know what a play is. It felt like anger at the injustice of it all. Or am I just jealous?

Yes, life would be easier, I wouldn't have to spend hours of preparation figuring out ways to do things on a shoestring. Yes, it would be nice simply to turn up and teach with everything laid on. But I'm much more useful to society, and to myself, dragging my country kids kicking and screaming all the way towards something they may never get the chance to do ever again, towards an experience of the sublime. I want them to feel the weightless timelessness of the inner space art can take them to. I want them to be transported by their own imagination. And you don't need stuff to do it — just a mind and a heart.

8th November

Rainfall last month: Not quite an inch

Jobs for this month:

- Sow — 1st & 2nd or 29th & 30th: Pigeon peas, Roi de Carouby snow peas, Scarlet Runner beans, tomato, Lipstick capsicum, Turkish Orange aubergine, Snowball cauliflower. 9th–11th; turnips, carrots, leeks, beets. 24th & 25th: broccoli, basil, lettuce, celery, parsley, silverbeet, cabbage, Chou Moulier kale.
- Move chooks at end of the month, & plant bed with corn & pumpkin from compost heap.
- Years 8, 9,10 marking — report cards.

My table is littered with flowers, video equipment, an empty bottle of vodka, two empty glasses and an overflowing ashtray. A pair of extremely uncomfortable high heels lie kicked off under a chair. Obviously, it was a big night. I stagger to my feet feeling like I've just risen from a shallow grave with a pickaxe embedded between my eyes. How did this still life manage to arrange itself? I retrieve the memory of a similar feeling of disconnectedness and reconstruct the brief image of the morning after the birth of my son when I woke up to garlands of flowers. That folds out into a hospital ward, a labour room — and then I remember where I really am and what I've just been through.

Opening night. *Oh, what a night!*

It's over and the kids were brilliant! There's nothing words can say about it — except that it went off!

My daggy, loud, ordinary, brash little country kids transformed themselves at the last minute into a cast. They all peaked at the right moment, and for an hour were suspended together in the world they had created. Sure, there were a couple of glitches — a hilarious moment where someone didn't turn up for their cue on time and the wayward curtain with a mind of its own — but what they did together was astonishing. Between them, they constructed and flew a time machine. The story was transferred from the playwright's mind directly into theirs, polished till they were all seeing and hearing it the same way. They poured their time and energy into its fuel tank, took it for a couple of test runs round the course to get the feel of it — worked out where the bumps and potholes were — and last night they let 'er rip. Now that they've reached their destination, they know where they've been — on a journey into themselves, and they've brought something out of their collective imagination to life. I'm so proud of them I could pop. It took till the wee hours to finally come down from the buzz.

Now I can reclaim my life and direct my energy back into my neglected garden. It's been suffering not only my absence, but the false promise of spring rain. I'm back to pumping. Because of my crook back, the corn I planted didn't go in on the fertile moon, and is stunted. The fruiting annuals that should have had rain to fill them with juicy plumpness are lean and small. Barely a month has gone by this past couple of years that has behaved as it should.

I realise that a food-bearing garden is not that important in the scheme of national agricultural output, we're not talking millions of dollars' worth of export revenue in jeopardy due to climate change and drought, but it means a lot to me. The investment is the same: proportionally, there's the same amount of labour involved and the same desired result — it's just that I haven't gone into debt and spent a fortune on diesel and seed and fertiliser and chemical soil supplements and pesticide and equipment to produce the same end as any other farmer — a living. There wouldn't be many farmers out there whose partners aren't working flat out, often off the property, teaching or working a small business in town to bring in some cash. The feeling of failure is the same, the sense of loss and futility equal.

I'm glad we didn't rush into any of the half a dozen cash-crop ideas we had when we first got here. I combed the market for niche crops, did countless sums, and looked into growing hemp, proteas, perhaps an annual vegetable, but all of them added up to large amounts of capital investment in plant, greenhouses, cold storage, seed or root stock and increased energy use, none of which we had the up-front finance for. And we are certainly in no position to go into debt, especially as it looks like the stuffing is about to come out of the global economy.

Even though it does rain here, we are still in drought because rainfall is unreliable and unpredictable. The climate may be subtropical, but if you grow, say, mangoes, and get heavy rain at the wrong moment, it takes with it all the flowering, and consequently no mangoes form. There is a hillside in a neighbouring valley where an unfortunate grower has bulldozed an established orchard. It is an ugly, tragic scar on the landscape that will take years to heal before he can try something different.

Had we put in a crop, this last month of no rain would have seen the fuel bill for pumping water eat into any profit margin. The thing with water is, if you are up high, there is a limit to how much you can harvest. It buckets down, sure, in swimming-pool volumes, but runs away to the flat immediately. Only the areas that are heavily mulched retain any residual moisture, but with thick mulch, you need a lot of rain to saturate it and seep down into the soil. Six of one, half a dozen of the other.

When I wanted to go to art school, my father nagged me relentlessly to choose art teaching instead: 'You want something to fall back on,' he'd say. As much as I still hate to admit it, he was right. Without the teaching work I can get here, life would be pretty lean. There is no money to be made from a small holding like ours. This self-sufficiency thing is so much harder than I ever imagined, being always at the whim of the fickle elements.

But things are nevertheless holding up in my little patch of dirt. I do my rounds, inspect the ground troops and harvest ripe vegetables. There are still creamy-fleshed broad beans swelling in their pods, the last of the sugarsnaps are still crisp, even if the leaves are brown and smutty from watering, and turnips are ready to pull. The Coven love the tops, and we get the bulbs. There's baby beetroot and red-veined silverbeet, and late-pick florets of broccoli may be tiny, but are delicious steamed up with carrots and then fried for about two seconds in butter with leeks. Tomatoes won't be long, as well as eggplants and capsicums if the weather warms up enough to make them set flower. Three eggs from the girls, basil for pesto, and a scoop from the feed bin for Mrs Mini.

But she's gone. Not a feather, no sign of a struggle, just gone, leaving her nest of cold, lonely eggs.

Forty abortions on my hands. What to do? We can't eat them, the hatch has already started. Consign them to the compost heap?

According to my livestock book, eggs can cope with cooling down a little — so they might still be alive! The more I read, the stronger my curiosity, and I decide to try to incubate them.

With a thermometer, a 40-watt light bulb, a foam box, and plenty of hope, they are soon installed on the bench in my kitchen, to be turned three times a day. Marking them with a cross on one side so I don't get confused, I can't help making the Easter connection.

In this unseasonably cool weather, it's tricky getting the temperature right. I have the light propped up on short blocks of wood over the box and will move them higher and lower to regulate its heat. The book mentions candling eggs. This means holding them in front of a light, to see if they have begun to form embryos. But all I can make out is a clear bubble of air or fluid, no idea which, and a darkness — rot? form? consciousness? I suppose the only thing to do is wait till we start to smell sulphur.

To make matters worse, when I checked the mail this morning there was this — with all the individual letters carefully cut out of the newspaper and stuck down to spell out:

Your birds are going to die!

I know who is responsible; in fact, I saw it being delivered. It's just a joke, from the only person who can't cope with the Minipecks' raucous warbling first thing in the morning: Joanna. It's the Minis' own fault: they take some perverse bird pleasure in performing their dawn chorus outside her bedroom window because they can be assured of the game of dodging the projectiles that rain down from her verandah. She keeps public service hours and they don't. I'm not sure how to break the news to her that forty more may be on the way. But she's right, birds do die around here, and if these survive they are doomed to become Tudor Turkeys.

Our first attempt at raising poultry to eat was a bit of a disaster. I bought a dozen meat birds from the local stock-and-feed supplier, who cleverly guarantees future sales by making seriously cute little fluffy chicks available for purchase by suckers like me, who will then spend a fortune on grain to raise them for the table. They are only a couple of days old when you buy them, and need not only special chick starter but all the hardware to go with it — almost worse than human babies for infant paraphernalia — chick drinker, brooder, feeder and a heat source. They keep practically the same hours as human babies too, alternately feeding and sleeping at about fifteen-minute intervals all night and day. We'd be lying in bed almost asleep when they'd wake up and start pecking, hence they became known as the Peckabirds. Really, birds should be called 'pecks'. I don't know where the English language got 'bird' from — it is utterly unonomatopoeic. Once old enough to leave the brooder, they progress to a slightly larger cage on the lawn beside the house, and finally to the static chook pen out in the garden.

Unfortunately, carnage, red of tooth and claw, was visited upon our pleasant valley in the form of a real-life predator, as opposed to the imaginary ones whipped up on the airwaves. Geoffrey, who had become attached to the Peckabirds, arrived home to find one of his little charges still warm, but headless and claw punctured on the ground, and the others traumatised and cowering under the chookhouse. He took to referring to this own-brand of rearing poultry as free-range falconry. You have to be Zen enough to intuit the precise moment of the kill, and lucky enough to interrupt proceedings so that the predator only gets the head, leaving the rest for the table. It's clean and costs little karma, but is wildly unreliable.

The addition of bird netting over their yard solved the problem of aerial attack, but then a couple of the smaller birds began to find it challenging to stand and walk. When a third began to stumble, tripping over large feet and using a wing to keep balance, I pulled all three out of the flock, fearing dire poultry diseases, most of which are pretty hideous. They'd had a *coccidiosis* scare when they were tiny, but this seemed more serious. I took them inside for some Florence Nightingale treatment in their own smelly box in the corner of the kitchen, but they seemed altogether too perky for sick chickens, so I called the vendor for advice.

Apparently, they should have reached optimum weight and been killed by that age. The stumbling thing is bred into them! Geoffrey had thought that they should be lean, clean health machines but every protein of their DNA only wanted to be fed. So back into the yard they went, to be supplied with a constant stream of scraps and corn. They never recovered the use of their legs — they just sat and ate, till it was our turn.

And it's not only our domestic birds that are doomed. Every year a family of magpie geese arrives to breed on the neighbour's dam in front of our house, and nest on an old stump sticking up out of the water in the shallows. They hang out in groups of three — a male, a female and a minder. I'm not sure of the minder's sex, but it is an effective method of making sure that at least one of the next generation makes it through to adulthood. They range right along the string of dams and I'm delighted to find them grazing in my front garden some mornings, honking to each other, shepherding their young among my pawpaw trees and pumpkin vines. They are very beautiful, large, swan-like birds, pied black and white, hence their common name.

Helen convinced Geoffrey that if he built an island pontoon on *her* dam, they might be encouraged to nest there, but so far they've resisted her offer. Don't know why, perhaps it's not a solid enough foundation and they can't trust the wavering, wobbling sensation of a floating platform. But I know where she's coming from because I *do* have a view of them nesting, and it is a large pleasure to watch the goslings take their first tentative leap of faith into the dam, and see them lined up for swimming lessons behind their mother.

They start out with five or six progeny but, as the season progresses, one by one the brood decreases to two or three, whether by snakes or goannas or birds of prey, or that bloody feral cat. In the end they manage to fly off, to wherever it is they go with a couple of offspring in tow.

Last year disaster struck. The juveniles were almost fully fledged when a pack of dogs was heard savaging them. No one is certain whose dogs they were — could have been a pack of ferals from the other side of the ridge, and we sometimes hear dingoes whooping on moonlit hunting nights — but the honking panic and trauma was felt all down the valley. None of the babies survived. We are all hoping that they'll return, but why would they?

Still, predators have got to make a living too, just as they do in the free market economy, and, as we know, it is the high-flyers who make off with the spoils and get away with it somehow. Bottom feeders of the criminal classes — I have a feral cat in mind here — end up in prison if you can catch them, but the majestic eagle is blameless — something to do with its magnificence, its poise, its grace, its nobility. The result is the same, dead and consumed domestic livestock, but what a way to go, eh? I watch the raptors soar on the thermals above our hills, usually in pairs, only the slightest adjustment of a feather necessary to keep them aloft, practically motionless, and then wings taper for a dive and — *pheouw* — they plummet, deft and accurate, at some unsuspecting small creature target: a joey, rabbit, lizard, bandicoot, feral cat!

I was out in the yard with Geoffrey one afternoon when one zeroed in just above us — it sounded like a jet, the low pressure beneath the lift of its wing cracking against the sound barrier. Another time, a year or two ago, we were fishing down on the Noosa River when a storm blew up. We took our dinghy out of the water to shelter under, when a sea eagle flew directly at us. It was actually after a fish, but had not factored our position and the relative weight of its potential catch into its calculations. It dipped its claws into the water in one arching swoop, and heading directly at our heads, saw us at the last moment and swerved. I can't forget the look of complete contempt in its eye as it avoided us with a last-minute evasive manoeuvre.

The Minipecks know they are there, though. Occasionally I see them standing perfectly still on the lawn, heads cocked in the same direction, each with one eye looking up. And sure enough, a pinpoint of stationary outspread wings is circling, coasting beyond the clouds.

We saw a stealth bomber last month. Well, either a stealth bomber or an alien spacecraft. Whatever it was it was, stationary in the sky above the Maroochydore airport without any landing lights on.

We'd been to a wedding. I go to an excellent masseur for my crook back. He is sweet and good hearted and really does have healing hands, and seems to generate a positive energy. I always feel improved by his touch, so it is worth the drive down to Coolum for treatment. We have become friends, and he invited us to his nuptials. It was an outdoor affair with a celebrant, under a shelter at Point Perry overlooking the ocean. Guests holding rainbows of balloons and parti-coloured gerberas followed the couple along the path leading to the point and gathered to watch them get hitched. Only a few passing punters were confused by the sight of two ecstatic beautiful young men holding hands, surrounded by their adoring family and friends.

I can't remember the last time I was at a wedding where the emotion was so deep and abiding, and the triumph so political. It's not that long ago you could be bashed for that kind of thing up here. Afterwards they held a party in the penthouse of one of the towers along the beachfront. It was still light, with the sun low in the west behind the ranges, and we had an all-round view. The tower is near the airport. We sat cracking black 9/11 jokes on the balcony as planes banked over the ocean for final approach, seemingly directly at our building. Then there it was. Geoffrey saw it first and called me over to check it out. A black, triangular form in the western sky.

Perhaps it was the angle of the sun, and our height above the ground that made it visible, but whatever it was, it was most certainly not a domestic aircraft. It moved, but not smoothly; rather, it appeared to reduce in size incrementally, but maintain its shape in jumps. Then it vanished into the void, just like that. Others saw it, too. Spy plane seemed to be the concensus on what it was, though I'm not sure what could possibly be worth spying on at a holiday resort.

I've asked around. The editor of a local magazine who publishes the findings of the Gympie UFO desk, among a wealth of other out-there information, was decidedly under-impressed — 'There's lots of those around here.' It's apparently a fairly common occurrence to see strange objects in the sky. In fact, I've even heard talk of serious enthusiasts out in the sticks who've built landing pads in their paddocks in the hope that ET may some day call Australia home. I suppose it's because the sky is a lot bigger out here. Nowhere to run, nowhere to hide. So from now on I'm going to be keeping a more wary eye on the heavens — just in case.

I have a beautiful view of their northern expanse from our front verandah, framed below by a railing covered in a tangle of night-scented jasmine which climbs up two wooden uprights that support the awning above. We can sit and watch the full moon rise, the arc of her slow-motion dance bounded by this verdant proscenium arch. It has been too cold to stay out in the night air without sleeves till now, so this evening the plan is to sit in the front stalls in the milder weather and enjoy the show. Our soundtrack is Arvo Pärt, following an overture of the night shift clocking on: frogs, crickets and the myriad unseen, unnamed, unknown creatures of darkness. But first, I need to turn the eggs.

Pick. Peck. Poke. Pock.

I hear it first, ear cocked above the mouth of the box. Then an almost imperceptible triangular crack in the smooth porcelain surface of first one, then another. But I'm not convinced till I hear peeping from inside. They are alive! My baby birds are percussively singing themselves into being. I can't believe it! Then a flap of shell pushes out and I can see a beak, nostrils, and the *peep* becomes a definite *cheep*. A crack extends round the widest part in slow motion. With each breath, the chick's muscles grow stronger and can't be confined any longer. Then a head pops out, blinks and looks around at its new reality.

I've never seen an egg hatch before — well, I was there when my son was born, but not outside looking down on the miracle, like a god. I am witness to forty globes of possibility that have, since their first stirring, graduated to probability of life. I can barely contain my joy and Geoffrey is having a hard time of it, too. I think we are crying, but it feels like wonder as we watch — how amazing, how astonishing, how beguiling life is.

My neck aches from the birthing centre. I've been at it two days, midwiving my clutch of Nanopecks. They don't actually need my help, it's just that the whole thing is so completely astonishing that I can't tear myself away. One minute breakfast, the next, a squirming, glistening, quivering baby bird. Each one perfect and autonomous, and the drama of each hatching equal to all the others. I'm watching number twenty-eight emerge while Richard Dawkins gives a lecture on the radio about his *God Delusion*, trying to explain why intelligent design is silly, why religion is the work of a fairly stunted imagination, and smashing the Old Testament into so many shards of broken eggshell.

Looking at the inexplicable contents of my incubator, I can find no meaning, no morality, no reason and no point in asking myself which comes first — the chicken or the egg? They are the same thing. A mystery. Neither science nor religion can come up with a reasonable explanation for life. I don't think humans ever will. Both demand a leap of faith in ideas I can't see or touch, so I'm content to be simply amazed that in one hand I can hold an egg, and in the other an animated, warm, breathing creature.

By the arrival of number thirty, I'm thinking that the chicken *is* the egg, and it is merely sloughing off its calcium skin, like the reptile it resembles — a little fin-flapping turtle — only slightly further up the energy scale, or as Darwin might suggest, further up the evolutionary ladder.

The alchemy begun by the constant body heat of Mrs Mini and continued artificially by my wish, has made these contained blobs of protein coalesce into what they are now. The first out are robust and alert, inquisitive and already eating and drinking as the last few make finishing touches to themselves inside. Only a handful remain to hatch now; the box is an infestation of rippling, teeming energy. A miracle; something out of nothing, out of nowhere into being; sprung from the void.

Everyone is eager to see the miracle of my virgin birth — Christopher stands on a chair, peering over the edge hoping to see it actually happen, my sister has brought her daughter to have a look, my parents snap photos. It's not hard to imagine how mystified the Madonna must have been about all the kerfuffle over such an ordinary thing as the birth of her child.

In all the excitement, I've entirely overlooked how I'm going to feed all these hungry mouths and where they will live. In eight months these little fluff balls will be chicken-sized creatures that will shit, eat and take up a lot of space — and then be slaughtered by me for their meat. I'll do the evil deed, which is only fair, considering it is always poor Geoffrey who finds the carcasses after the predators have had their fill. Like Mrs Mini's wing, which he found up in the triangle paddock.

I arrive at school to find I'm not the only one with baby photos. The preschool teacher is the proud foster mother of a brand new foal and is eagerly passing snaps around the staffroom, stealing my thunder. She, like me, is on the verge of tears, still shaky from the emotion of it. But I've also got the emotional comedown of the play to contend with — no less of a miracle.

I was alone in the delivery room for the past ten weeks, but now the baby is out, being passed around, discussed in the community among parents, and I'm enjoying the compliments and their pride in the kids' achievement, the praise and shared pleasure. I've almost completely forgotten how difficult it was, as you do with birth; how sharp the contractions, how confronting the pain. Which is just as well really, because now I have to deal with the afterbirth. There are assignments to be handed in, the little kids' performances to present, and the looming problem of keeping the big kids concentrated on the rest of the term now that they are famous and think they should be lolling about a pool, wearing sunglasses and signing autographs.

I filmed the play for them and spent a couple of nights cutting two cameras' worth of shots together, one long, taking in the whole stage, and Geoffrey's close-up footage from the front to one side. I put titles and credits on it and ran it during class for them to see themselves performing. A lot of their peers who didn't make it to the show sat in and watched, too. About a quarter of the way through, one boy asked, 'How long does this go for?'

I said, 'An hour, but if you are bored you are welcome to leave.'

Instead, he shook his head in disbelief and replied, 'How did they remember it all?'

The cast exchanged self-satisfied grins, chuffed to be blowing their friends away like that.

There's about two weeks of school left, then my contract finishes. A replacement performing arts teacher has been found but I've been asked if I want to take on a new contract to teach English full-time for a full year. I've been keeping this to myself till now, but the deputy wants an answer on Monday and I have to bite the bullet with Geoffrey. He's got a fairly good handle on how much I'm in love with the kids and how much pleasure I get from teaching them, even though it takes up so much of my attention — and that's only two days a week. Imagine, five days a week, day in day out. It's been driving me nuts and I'm relieved, finally, to share my indecision. It's the main topic of conversation over dinner.

I lay all the cards on the table, all rehearsed and arranged into pros and cons: We could save some money; but do we really need that much? We manage on what we have; but it would be good to stash some away for a rainy day. It would be full-time, and not just the days, but all that preparation time. He'd need to take on the added garden chores, and the cooking, and shopping; but his hands are full with the farm. Would he cope? I'm chuffed to be asked — it's a big boost to my confidence to return to the profession after all this time and be offered the job — but there's still a hell of a lot of professional development to do to get up to speed, and I don't have twenty years of collected materials up my sleeve; I'd have to start from scratch, and that would take up all my spare time on the weekends, too.

He brings up the travel time and the cost of petrol. The school is too far away. In about six months we'd have to go into debt to buy a new car, because that drive would kill the Valiant. Though it guzzles gas, I love that car. It is a classic, and the insurance is much cheaper because of that. Besides, part of the reason for moving here is to reduce our carbon footprint. Two and a half tanks of petrol a week just to get to work and back is an almost unthinkable waste of energy.

Mainly, though, it's about the kids. Drama is one thing, but I don't think I believe that core subjects like English should be taught by fly-by-nighters like me — all care but ultimately no responsibility. These kids need continuity, someone who knows them well and lives in their community with them, as part of their lives. But I've just spent almost a year getting to know them, and to leave them now, just as I have gained their trust to the point where I can actually teach them properly, seems an unthinkable waste of time. Teaching is personal. You can't tell a teenager anything till you have earned their respect, and that is impossible without understanding who they are.

Contractors receive no holiday pay. We are a cheap, flexible casual workforce to the department, but just a passing parade of strangers to the kids. It may be a 'cost-effective method of delivering education outcomes', whatever that means, but it is not a particularly ethical way of providing an actual education. The system, I say, has to stop staffing schools on quotas of bums on seats and start attracting young teachers to rural schools with reasonable pay and housing. It's a question of duty of care.

He pours more red wine into my glass, as I continue with my soliloquy. A young English teacher with a family should be placed there in a full-time, salaried position. I can deal with the short-term contractor role if it is a stop-gap, but not when it is a departmental expediency. Unless someone draws the line and refuses to be a cog in the system, it won't even know that something rotten is eating away at its core. But then again, it's English, I'm trained for that. It might not take up as much time — still — five days, only the weekends for the garden. No, I'm too busy.

By now, with a sip or two more, I've convinced myself that by turning it down, I'm making an ethical political statement, with the best interests of the children at heart. But my soapbox melts and my feet hit the ground when Geoffrey finally gets a word in:

'Remember what we came here for? If you wanted to work forever for other people, you could have stayed in Sydney. Do you really want to go back there? What about your own work?'

My own work? What work? He better than anyone knows that I have done nothing towards this alleged 'own work' ethic. He's watched me piss a whole year up against the wall, watched me polish cutlery rather than actually engage in anything to do with 'my own work'. I'm almost angry with him for bringing up my obvious and complete failure in getting off my arse and doing something, anything, that might vaguely resemble the product of an internal passion. But I'm more angry with myself, and try hard not to choke on the tears I can feel welling up, and agree:

'Quite right, it is a ridiculous idea. Of course, I will turn it down.'

He clears the dishes away, and as he clatters about in the kitchen washing up I take up a pile of assignments that need to be marked before tomorrow. Later I'll try to figure out how to use the computerised reporting system into which I have to enter all the marks. It will take me most of the night to get my head around how to work a spreadsheet. I keep wondering if I'm doing the right thing turning the job down. Am I only being an egomanic in allowing myself to think the kids need me? Am I letting them down by deserting them for my own selfish desire?

I have to admit that six months in the education system has reminded me of why I developed such a 'poor attitude to authority', as my own school reports complained. Public education is reduced to a political football. Students and teachers, the most central to the whole enterprise, are paradoxically the most marginalised when it comes to decision making. We stand there, rooted in the system as the swells and tides of rhetoric sweep over us. Teachers are the most important other adults in a kid's life for twelve years; you'd think that would be worth more than an economic bottom line to a society.

I'm marking the critical analysis essays by my drama kids. They have to tell me all about the experience of putting on the play using, in correct context, the drama vocabulary we've picked up in the last few months. There is a vast range in their capacity to communicate; from a fluent three pages of confident prose, to a half-page of barely legible three-word responses which are supposed to be paragraphs. They really could do with an English teacher, but the play has at least given them something to write about authoritatively. Halfway through the pile I get to a paper written from somewhere in the middle of the range and find a little glittery purple-inked note at the end that dissolves me into floods of conflicted tears:

Thank you so much for helping us do the play.
It is the best thing I have ever done in my whole life.
I will never forget it.

summer

9th December

Rainfall last month: Four inches — yeay!

Jobs for this month:

- Sow — 7th & 8th: leeks, Cylindra beets, carrots. 26th & 27th: broccoli, basil, cabbage, celery, lettuce, parsley, silverbeet. 30th & 31st: Mortgage Lifter tomatoes, Udamalapet eggplant, capsicum, Rondo de Nice zucchini, cucumber, Giant Russian sunflower.
- Pull tomatoes & replace with beans.
- Watch for mildew as honeydew, rockmelons & watermelons are setting fruit.
- Research fly traps for peaches or get over peaches.
- Get rid of jumping ants under peach tree.
- Make up the spare bedroom for Therese. (Lay in medical supplies!)

It's still not hot yet. Something weird is going on if we get to December and don't wilt by 9 am. Either the timber plantation has created its own micro-climate in the valley, or global warming is cool. No one's complaining, but my skin memory of December expects it to become putrid at any moment. We're still wearing covers on the bed at night, unheard of at this time of year. The Coven is covered at the moment too, since the arrival of Fluffy.

Fluffy is a showy jungle fowl rooster, about two feet tall with startling long spurs on the back of his legs, and brilliant iridescent green-black, red and golden-orange plumage, and his comb is rigid and fleshy as a stiffy. He's a very attractive man, if you are a chicken. And like any toy boy, what he lacks in wit, he more than makes up for in strut and first impressions. He's even turned Twenty into a submissive little chickibabe.

He arrived courtesy of a stranger who must have seen the chook dome from the road and decided that we'd appreciate inheriting his rooster. He was moving to town and couldn't take his livestock with him, certainly not a rooster anyway. He had one of those Ned Kelly beards and numerous tattoos, making Geoffrey feel disinclined to argue about it, so a couple of days later Fluffy materialised in the dome, to the complete delight of the happy, eyelash-batting Coven.

I can sleep through a rooster crowing at 2 am, 3 am, 4 am, kookaburras pissing themselves laughing at 5 am, and Minipecks squee-squawking at 6 am, but some people only have to suspect the presence of a rooster nearby and they'll lie awake all night waiting for it to go off. The author of the death threat isn't yet wise to the identity of the new alarm clock in the valley. If Fluffy does make too much noise and drive everyone nuts, Christmas is just round the corner and he is almost as big as a turkey.

Now that school is over and I'm no longer plagued by the indecision of the last month, life has resumed its quietude and time is mine again. While I read, or write my diaries at the big table, I feel Geoffrey concentrating on his endless projects in the other room. He is one of the most useful humans ever to have the opposing thumb. He can fabricate anything, is endlessly practical, always busy, and not given, as I am, to leaning on the verandah railing for half an hour to watch changing light shade the eucalypts from pastel yellow to powdery blue. Even in the evenings there is an ongoing project, usually to do with his little boats.

In his youth he was a sailor, and he still loves messing about in boats. A poet's budget doesn't stretch to racing a maxi yacht, but because he can make just about anything from scratch, he races little ones — radio-controlled one-metre yachts. He spends weeks fashioning a hull, laying up and glassing its form, sanding and polishing, making tiny deck fittings, rigging with fishing-line trace, and cutting sails.

His obsession is contagious and I'm into it now too, even though I have no experience of big boat sailing. It's taken me two years to learn the rules of racing and get my boat handling skills to a level where I can sail in the fleet without screwing up the other skippers' race. It is the one thing we do together that keeps us from being total hermits. Once a fortnight we load up the boats and sail boxes and drive down to the coast to race at our local club against some of the best skippers in the national fleet, among them ex-Olympic big boat champions. The competition is fierce, considering that we are sailing toy boats. The only difference between sailing a maxi and these Stuart Little ones is a couple of squillion dollars — everything else is the same.

Last year I was still struggling with the physics of it so that I could tune my own boat, and spent a lot of time trying to get my head around vortices and oscillation. I'd been reading one of Geoffrey's books on the subject of how a hull moves through the water and how to calculate boat speed and the like, when a big clanging penny dropped. Water doesn't move forward with the wave, as it seems to at the beach; rather, it moves up and down as the wave passes through it. I tried to picture it in my mind and, out of nowhere, a question formed:

What would happen if a section of the seabed suddenly fell away?

Geoffrey drew some diagrams for me, unfolding the details, and then we thought nothing more of it till a couple of days later when those very same diagrams turned up in the newspapers in the aftermath of the Asian tsunami. I felt a shiver when I realised I'd already imagined it.

Spookily, the animals there had sensed the tsunami coming and headed for the hills but the people hadn't. What are animals tuned into that we have lost the capacity to recognise? It makes you think and wonder: what if we, with our big brains, are actually at the bottom of the evolutionary ladder? We aren't really that clever, we need language to communicate for starters — the cows don't. There are times when the steers watch us harvesting the oranges they can't reach, and maybe they wish they had hands and could climb a ladder, but they've got plenty of time and would have all the oranges by just waiting, if we didn't get to them first. They also know, long before I do, that the weather is about to go weird.

My Minipecks are behaving strangely — fluttering and running round in circles beneath their tree. A crisp anvil of cloud is rising in front of the afternoon sun, making things ominously dark. Then an eerie greenish-orange light floods into the valley, drenching everything in bright acid-pink for a moment. But the Minis don't flap up — they stay on the ground out in the open. And the chooks are all pressed against the far side of the dome, not under the shelter over it, but right up against the wire.

All I can see is that it's shaping up to be a classic December afternoon storm. The animals must be spooked by the thunder rumbling like ravenous hunger in the swollen, distended belly of this one. And the bilious green beneath its purple density suggests it might contain hail. I resign myself to the possibility and hope the larger trees that surround the garden will break its fall before it destroys six months' work.

We hear the rain shearing down the valley before it arrives and see the trees on the hillside above us bent almost double in the face of the wind. But I'm still not concerned. Storms usually blow in from the southwest and shriek harpy-like above — we are down low and they are generally deflected off the hills as they eddy through, pinball-bouncing off the ridges.

Standing on the verandah in the lee of it, with the house at our backs, I'm caught up in the storm's exhilarating rush. This one is a cracker. Lightning, simultaneous with its deafening explosion, splits the air. And the wind! I could take off into it, aloft on the full force of the front, like the black cockatoos that surfed this one. Weightless and ecstatic at the height of it, I hear the cyclonic roar of a vacuum of low pressure sucking air into itself, feel the skin-prickle of its magnetic force, and wonder if we'll lose the roof.

Suddenly, the Minipecks' roosting branch snaps and hits the deck — right on top of them. There is nothing to do but hope they haven't been killed. The dome is holding even though it is light and I haven't pegged it down, and the entire sodden Coven is huddled up under Fluffy.

The storm cell then lifts up its billowing skirts, leaps over the northern ridge and is gone. And one by one the Minis pick their way out from under the foliage of the fallen branch.

It is nightfall by the time the wind dies down and the rain stops completely. No damage to speak of, unless you are a Minipeck and your roost has been blown clean away.

Next morning my parents arrive way too early for visiting hours. They've been out surveying the aftermath and, because they couldn't raise me on the phone (I'd forgotten to plug it back in after the storm), were worried. With childlike, wide-eyed enthusiasm they describe the devastation down in town, and tell us we won't be able to get out because only 4WD access is possible. I don't believe them, it didn't seem that bad, but when we go to town soon after, we take the chainsaw just in case.

Three enormous gums down, power lines snapped like broken rubber bands, a carpet of leaves stripped from the now-naked limbs of trees; this must be where she touched down hard after sailing out of our valley. There's no way the Valiant could negotiate the obstacles and drive into the sludge on the verge of the road where my dad carved his track earlier. Nothing for it but to cut a way through.

Reou. Reou. Reouwwwwnnn.

I love the sound of a chainsaw in the morning. From every dwelling within earshot, a battalion of similarly armed blokes emerges, like blowflies on the whiff of rotten meat. We stand at a safe distance and watch aghast as three heroes in thongs carve and buzz their way through a fallen gum at waist height. An hour later the road is cleared, but I wonder how many chainsaw injuries will turn up at Emergency later in the day.

Town is a mess and a couple of the streets down near the lake are write-offs. Cars flattened, trees in living rooms, roofs off, and the botanical gardens lie in ruins. What a perfectly awesome tantrum the storm has thrown down here on the flat: everywhere is the debris of brokenness, like the contents of a kitchen smashed against the wall in domestic fury. But it's silly to personify a storm — it's just a storm — your regular, garden-variety act of God.

I'm no stranger to acts of God. Brisbane in 1974 still looms large in my memory: sunken suburbs with only the tiny apex of roofs visible, snakes strung in power lines, and my father ferrying ice in his boat to friends stranded by the flood. The whole city seemed permanently pissed because fresh water was scarce and refrigeration non-existent: the blokes did the noble thing and drank all the beer on hand before it got hot.

And I was in the big Sydney hailstorm in 1999. At the time I had a little black dog. She was edgy and weird for the whole day, but because she was part kelpie and perpetually edgy and weird I didn't think anything of it till just before the storm struck. Though all was quiet she ran from one end of the house to the other, yelping and jumping up at the barred windows and the closed front door. She wanted out of there. Eventually, unable to make me see sense she sat at the back door casting anxious looks at the greening sky and back at me as if I was mad. Just before I heard the turbine of the hail front approach, she was momentarily rigid — then she pulled her tail between her legs and fled to the space under the stairwell. In about two minutes, when the storm struck, my son and I joined her.

Come to think of it, I must have known something was up. I had planned to go out that evening to a film launch, and had organised takeaway pizza for Evan, who would watch TV with the dog till I got home. I didn't go. For some reason I felt unable to drag myself away from him.

That storm was really terrifying. I've experienced big ones in Brisbane that take out every window on the presenting side of the city, but to be in Sydney in a hailstorm was new to me — the roofs are tile, not corrugated iron which only dints. How was I supposed to know that the mounting pile of orange shards mixed with the half-brick-sized lumps of ice filling up the backyard was my roof? Or know that within a couple of hours the ice that had collected in the ceiling would melt, stream down the walls and light fittings, and leave us with no shelter?

To my great relief, an armour-plated knight leapt to the rescue. Geoffrey had me waterproof by the following day, having found the last sheets of corro available in town before the promise of insurance jobs locked it all down with a spiralling price hike. It took the SES three days to arrive with tarps, by which time the elderly residents who'd been camping under their stairwells were already slowly dying of shock and exposure. That long-term death toll never made it to the papers. A year later, almost every house in my street had a new owner, a building approval for a new attic bedroom in the ceiling, and my insurance premium went through the roof.

They're funny things, natural disasters. They tend to bring out the best in people — a generosity born out of a kind of there-but-for-the-grace-of-god empathy. The tsunami did it on a gigantic media-manipulated scale. An overtly mourning West with its big, empathetic heart on its sleeve could imagine itself stretched out on a beach sipping coolers served by coolies, and threw millions at the unfolding disaster. Lucky it was Christmas, with all that goodwill towards fellow man splashing around.

A big media spectacle can really get those empathy valves flowing, especially if it comes with a benefit concert and famous performers and fireworks and wristbands that mark you as having done your bit for the cause.

By the height of the frenzy of goodwill, giving had become a competitive sport. A week later, in spite of all its technology and can-do, quick-fix best intentions, the West was astonished to find that people can't eat cash.

People once put money in the plate every Sunday. I did it myself as a child: dropped my reluctant twenty-cent piece onto the wide, shallow, green-felt-lined wooden bowl being passed along the pews. Its dull thud equalled one sausage roll, a red ice block and a fist-sized bag of snakes, cobbers and ripe raspberries.

Sunday school was weekend childminding, as far as I could tell. My parents rarely went to church. It was strictly births, deaths and marriages with them, because Sunday was the only day they had to spend any time together when Dad was actually awake. But I went to them all; Methodist, Baptist, C of E (all there were in my white-bread Brisbane suburb, back then), depending on which neighbour would take us and bring us back. We'd have to get dressed up and, as the eldest, I held onto the cash. I had a twenty-cent coin, and my sisters a ten-cent and a five-cent, in descending order of height. My favourites, however, were the Cattle Ticks. I never knew the word was *Catholic* till I started hanging out with Italian kids in North Queensland.

Carla's house was as shocking as the inside of somebody else's undies drawer. The whole living room was a fantastic votive shrine crammed with plug-in sacred bleeding hearts that lit up and glowed red, walls hung with crosses and reproductions of the Italian masters' Virgins. I was hooked when I saw the insides of their churches and stopped calculating what I was missing for my money. The theatre was worth it; the spookiness of incense and the mumbled jumble of Latin I didn't understand. I convinced myself that if He found out I wasn't one of them, at least I'd paid the entry fee, and wouldn't be struck by lightning.

One of the last things we did before leaving Sydney was to go to St Mary's — headquarters — for midnight mass. The cathedral on Christmas Eve — now there's a spectacle. Soft candlelight, flesh-hued sandstone interior soaring to a complexity of arches, plumes of perfumed incense mounting up, glowing brassy notes of trumpet, and heartbreaking angelic boy-soprano voices aloft an overtone of baritone drone, garlands of white lilies; beauty upon beauty.

It is pure time travel to feel transported across centuries of ritual and drama and solemn reverence, and it gets me every time. And it's a rare opportunity to sing in a mass of voices — Catholics are great singers. There must have been two thousand souls crammed into that magical space that night, all buoyed up by the shared hope of transcending earthly existence. Well, that's why I was there anyway.

As the crowd swelled, I felt open, lighter on my feet, suspended in the benign, smiling goodwill that emanated from it. Swept up by the vibration of the music, the loveliness of the space, I prepared to lose myself in the singularity of common resonance.

We were all warm and fuzzy and about to contemplate the miracle of life when some old white-bearded guy with the voice of Yahweh took to the podium with a litany of pre-emptive strikes that Isaiah's vindictive Father intended to visit on the Babylonians. Then he prophesied:

'For unto us a child is born, unto us a son is given: and the government shall be upon his shoulder; and his name shall be ... Prince of Peace.'

Two thousand years after they anointed this Prince (peace be upon him), nothing's changed, except now it's not God doing the smoting.

I don't entirely understand my aversion to organised religion, but my early contact led me to art-school immersion in the advertising billboards of Western Christianity. I am awash with its mystical and theological imagery, even though I just can't bring myself to believe in that finger-pointing, white-bearded guy on the cloud. The pitch is brilliant, but it has never compelled me to buy. Maybe it's because I'm Anglo-Australian: I've never had an invasion force rain depleted uranium on my city, never had my child stolen from me, never starved, never required a larger thing to believe in than life itself. I understand why people go there, but as much as I wish I could come to terms with its contradictions and insistence on blind faith, just can't do it myself.

Or maybe my lack of faith stems from the discovery, in my late teens, of the arts as a workable spiritual equivalent. They have since formed the core of how I make sense of the world. Pictures, plays, stories and music have always been the sermons I listen to, my sacred texts of ways to comprehend existence. So far, receiving the benediction of imagination has done it for me.

But now, leaving that world has left me feeling its lack. I miss my participation in the life of the soul, and teaching has reminded me — I miss that work, my evangelical tambourine-thumping *alleluia* of good news about a brilliant new novel, a new artist, a new resonant voice. In the city it was my meaning, my centre, and I feel the loss like a hollow ache.

I'm not the only one. Seems that the church is losing its foothold out here in the country, too. Congregations are in decline. All the pretty little wooden churches raised by the hearts and hands of devoted parishioners are closing, due to lack of interest, or meaning, or connection. They are being sold up and redeveloped, and their altars sit gathering dust in country sheds —

dismantled by the very people who so lovingly arranged for their consecration, in the hope that some day someone might find a use for them.

In the meantime, a local Buddhist carpenter has built a portable stupa that can be towed on a box trailer round the hinterland. It's been consecrated by a nun and a monk with all sorts of deeply symbolic stuff inside it, so powerful that even just looking at a photo of it can make you deliriously happy.

Christopher is in a state of perfect bliss already, and he doesn't even know the stupa exists. What he knows is that there is only one more sleep till the day of loot, but he also understands there are certain rituals to be observed. There is no opening of presents on Christmas morning till Granny and Grandpa return from church. Then it is his job to hand out the parcels under the tree, and each must be opened one by one. He knows the big one will be last, and will have his name on it. He's also got a pretty good idea of what will be inside.

Every year Granny sends Geoffrey or Joe up into the shed to retrieve a carefully marked box that contains just the thing for Christopher at any given age. Helen still has, stashed away, every favourite toy played with by her own children. Just a dust-off, some new felt and a dab of glue, and it'll be good as new. Invariably, it is *the* toy that claims most of his attention. Last year, no amount of plastic whiz-bangery could compete with a refurbished pool table with marbles for balls and onion-bag pockets.

This year, Geoffrey and I are vying for the best handmade-gift award.

Christopher has played mini-golf somewhere and a couple of weeks ago arrived with a tiny drawing in the middle of a piece of paper which, though it looked like a fly, was actually a design for a mini-golf hole. When I questioned him, he pointed out that the fly's wing was a propeller, 'And it spins, and you hit the ball through the blades to get it into the hole on the other side,' which is, apparently, the fly's eye. I told him that if he wanted it to be real, his drawing needed to get a lot bigger than a fly, at least bigger than a golf ball, with all the bits that it needed to work joined together, and arrows, lots of arrows. His next attempt did look like a kind of a plan, so he and Geoffrey set about searching for parts up in the shed. It has taken them much of the last week, and now the yard is an obstacle course of piles of interconnected junk with numbered flags marking out the order of the holes, and Christopher is already a pro.

Actually, the award really belongs to the gift Geoffrey has made for me — an aviary for the once Nano- but now Micropecks. My chicks have grown out of their previous pen and Geoffrey has made a most sturdy structure, with a high perch, tin roof and a set of wheels so it can be moved round the yard to fresh grass. It is called the Coop D Ville, and now that they have the space, my little fledglings are teaching themselves to flap up to perch. Even our rooster, Fluffy, is not forgotten in the season of goodwill — this morning I found a noose draped over the dome with a bow and a card that reads:

Dear Fluffy,
Get stuffed and join us for lunch.

It was not signed.

He's relatively safe this time. A turkey is already defrosting, soon to be filled with sausage meat in one end and something equally delicious in the other. It will come to rest in front of Grandpa to be carved, while all the trimmings are served onto the good matching china. And, in line with Grandma's adherence to correct table manners, no elbows will come into contact with any part of the table.

Geoffrey will miss out this year — he's ill — but Therese is here and will eagerly take his place. His parents' generous table has wings that spread out to accommodate guests. There is an old custom that says to always welcome strangers, because you might find you are entertaining an angel. In the case of our friend Therese, this is entirely likely.

Therese and I have been for a walk up to the container paddock to see Diamonte — a calf she named six months ago for the white diamond blaze in the middle of its head. And we've seen Number One, who is vast with child. She is due any moment with her first-born. Perhaps she'll turn the tables on our festive season and have the humans adoring *her* miraculous progeny. We drop in on the way back to find Christopher idly flipping through an illustrated book of bible stories, killing time with Granny on her front verandah while she does a crossword. I look over his shoulder at the page he has open, at a picture of a tree with a snake in it. I ask him if he knows the snake's name is Satan. He does, of course, because he is six and knows everything already. Since he is now practically reading, I ask: 'Did you know that all the letters in Satan are the same as in Santa?'

He looks at me puzzled, but Helen, who's only been half-listening to our conversation, sits bolt upright in her seat and replies instead of him: 'No, I did not!'

I think I've blown Santa's chances this year of Christmas cake offerings left out for his late-night convenience. I doubt he will even be allowed on the property, now that the truth has been revealed in the Word.

We wander back home along our dirt lane, towards a lapis northern sky of heaped-up clouds, burnished copper by the bright setting sun at our backs. Therese is Catholic, with a lick of blarney on her tongue, but all she can manage is, 'Will you look at that?'

Ah, but in the way she says it, I get every emotion, and share her speechlessness at the beauty flooding in through our senses. There is no cause and effect, no need for a metaphor to explain its existence. The whole of creation is contained in this vibrating moment of perception:

Beneath the gilded dome
flaked leaf paper altar burn.
Collapse inward,
your garden of Eden unfolds
within the eye of God.

Pantheon of clouds stream o'erhead
past iris, tulip, pupil.
Bulb of all knowledge,
flickers in a half life so intense,
of ten million light years.

10th January

Rainfall last month: Five inches!

Jobs for this month:

- Sow — 4th, 30th & 31st: Balinese corn — at least 60 plants for beds 3 & 4.
- Move Coven to back garden.
- Propagate lemon grass for front garden edge.
- Take fig cuttings & propagate — try experimental planting.
- Start autumn seedlings off.
- Geoffrey working at the yabby farm.
- Cook up picnic tucker for State titles.

Geoffrey is back on his feet again. He's only got himself to blame. By example he'd taught Christopher to swig from the cold water bottle in the fridge, and what seemed to be merely a snotty cold in the child passed on and developed into fever and full-on bronchitis in poor Uncle Noisy, requiring all my newfound amateur medico skills. He recovered eventually but it put him behind in the preparation of his boat for the national titles. He's not confident, but he's paid the entry fee.

So this morning we loaded up the little boats and are off to the shore of a very near-empty dam just north of Brisbane. There are three days of it. Geoffrey's sister Liz is competing too, but I'm not sailing. I've volunteered to be an observer, which means I'll spend three days at the water's edge calling out contacts when boats collide. Skippers from all over the country will be there to see if they can beat the World Champion, an Australian from Melbourne.

On the highway heading south we pass two billboards. The first advertises Australia Zoo. There he is, the ghost of Steve, ever present among us, hugging a crocodile with a big, manic grin about as wide and menacing as Steve's. The second, advertising a new real estate development, shows an ordinary guy hugging a labrador in pretty much the same pose, with an equally wired grin.

Then further on, we come to the Steve Irwin Way. It doesn't seem to go anywhere — just past the Australia Zoo, but with those two billboards at the back of my brain, I'm making imaginary connections. My mind's camera continues down the Steve Irwin Way and arrives at an enormous, landscaped, gated entrance, signposted *Mythical Delusions: Gateway to the Great Australian Dream.*

It is guarded by concrete sculptures of wild animals, but inside, happy, smiling nuclear families with perfect teeth, play with gentle, golden, shampooed pets on manicured lawns.

The Big Australian Drive will lead out to a commercial service precinct where everything is BIG; the big bed, the big furniture barn, the big pool, the big car, the big DYI hardware centre, the big W, the big clean nuclear power plant. It'll have everything so the resident will never need to leave this green and pleasant democratic place.

You can tell it is democratic because everyone's house will be a mansion adorned in just enough variety of architectural features so that the homeowners can express their own individuality and tell them apart from one another. And there will be peace and prosperity, and a personal *en suite* for all. It doesn't exist yet, but you can bet your life the plans have already been lodged with the council …

Anyway, we are living in a state of post Steve Irwin traumatic stress disorder up here, and everybody feels it. We are almost as obsessed by the demise of Steve as we are by the Maroons. If I talk to the locals about his passing I have to be very sensitive to their loss. Practically everyone knew him as their mate, a great bloke who really loved his kiddies — and, you'll be reminded, Bindi is a millionaire in her own right! We may only have seen him once at the zoo, or on TV introducing his baby boy to a carnivorous reptile, or extolling the virtues of hugging animals that have no desire to hug back, but it's enough to forge an unbreakable bond of camaraderie.

When we arrive at the lake, I have to keep remembering to bite my tongue whenever mention is made of the great ex-Steve. Don't want to disconcert the boys, who are already setting up tents, fiddling with minute rigging adjustments and getting the feel of the course. There are only four female skippers in a fleet of seventy boats, but a couple of them are right up there in the A-fleet. Only twenty boats can sail at once, so the fleet is divided into heats. A desperate pitched battle ensues to be among the four boats at the front of B-fleet who'll be promoted to A in the next race, and not to be among the last placed four in A-fleet who'll be demoted to B.

I love these big regattas — an excellent excuse to pack a picnic lunch and be by a stretch of calm water under a big wide blue sky. We're not the only users today. I can hear a motor from the other side of the dam. The unmistakable rumble of an inboard-engined ski boat transports me back to similar January days in my childhood, when my parents took us to spots like this to water ski. I think I must have been about seven or eight when I first crouched between my dad's knees on my own pair of half-sized wooden skis and felt the boat pull us up, watching my ski-points waver and click against his big slickly varnished ones, and the miraculous sensation of skimming across the water alone when he let go. With model boating, the pleasure is as large, but these days I don't get wet.

Five, four, three, two, one, and on the bell, in unison, the little fleet heads into the wind, sails on hard. The skippers clustered on shore clutch their controls, aerials extended, bent on the progress of the tiny craft. All is quiet till the weaving, tacking melee converges on the top mark, then it's on:

'Don't go in there!'

'I'm inside you!'

'Stay up!'

'I'm under you!'

'Below you, 69!'

'Contact!'

'Protest!'

Ah, the gentle art of model yachting. You never hear the hailing from the shore in big boat racing, but here, rising up into the clear air, with all the intensity of a football scrum, it is practically the language of love.

But it's not looking good for 593, Geoffrey's sail number. He's at the back of the fleet in the seeding race, and D-fleet is a big hole to climb out of.

*   *   *

It is an amusing diversion, but I can't imagine ever being obsessed enough by sailing my toy boat to become good at it. Obsession is an interesting phenomenon. There's nothing positive about it. It takes you over, fills your thoughts and crowds your mind with its object. But to become virtuosic, one needs obsession. An elite athlete needs to be obsessed by winning, a politician by power, an artist by self-expression. My garden is my obsession, but what is its end? What will be the achievement of all the work and planning and possession?

There is no end to a garden. There is always next season, always the next rotation, always another variety to plant and taste. It is utterly ephemeral and in one season, if left to itself, the wound I've dug will heal over, first weeds, then lantana, then the odd tree will sprout and take hold, and the earth will swallow this garden back into itself. It leaves no material evidence except its sensual, pleasurable procession, its ever-changing layout, its fluid composition, and cyclical change.

It's time to take the Coven cross-country again to the back garden, and this time Fluffy needs to be moved too, and is not happy about being bundled up in a hessian bag. I'm still wary of his spurs and not prepared to take any chances. I have cleared the waiting bed of the human food: Chioggia beets, amazing with their red and white boiled-lolly stripes; the last of the red-veined Ruby chard; and crimp-frilled Vertus cabbage. The rest is for the Coven, including a patch of lush alfalfa going to seed in a blanket of purple.

Fruit and vegetables should be sold with an image of their blossom attached to the price tag. Lettuce blooms in tiny yellow buttery curls, aubergine in drooping fuzzy-felted mauve and pink. Rocket erupts into a froth of pale cream, brown-centred pinwheels, and snow-pea flowers, pink, white and red, take on a darker hue as the petals wither and cling to the pod forming in their midst. Even the humble potato flower is a delight.

The only thing that doesn't seem to flower is our Black Genoa fig tree. Instead, little buds form on its sticky sappy branches, and swell into an embarrassment of blushing fruit. Apparently, the fruit is actually the flower, growing inside out: no wonder it is always associated with the female sex. Black genoas grow well here, so I am taking cuttings to get a productive number of trees going. Perhaps, after all, there is a cash crop that we can grow. So far it has only been bothered by an infestation of black grubs which devour the leaves, sucking all the moisture out from between the veins and leaving papery lace behind. But they can be managed by collecting the infested leaves and feeding them to the chooks. The grubs don't seem to damage the fruit, and if I can avoid a monoculture planting, fig trees might just do okay.

When the Coven is settled, I'll spread a thin layer of mulch on the bed where they've been. I'm not planting into this one. I'm letting the weeds come up to mine the deeper soil for nutrients, and will mow them down before they seed and dig the clippings into the soil. The front beds are still a long way from conditioned enough to grow anything much.

Summer has finally kicked in. Any physical work has to be done before the sun gets up over the towering camphor laurel to the northeast because by then it is sweltering. The Coven spends its day unable to do anything but stand panting, wings held out from their bodies to cool the down beneath their feathers. I drape the dome with hessian on days like this and hose it so it works like air conditioning, not that there's any breeze to speak of till late afternoon.

Now the dank, airless whiff of decay pervades every room in the house. The season of mildew, steamy damp, and fly-stung fruit — seething unseen on the kitchen bench, till it bursts open, rippling with maggots — is accompanied by the incessant groaning, bitching and moaning of the fridge.

My fridge can't deal with this weather. I bought it second-hand, a good deal, apparently; nothing wrong with it, till its European energy efficiency comes up against weather like this. It clunks and drones and shudders in the heat, pining for the fjords, and sails very close to becoming an ex-fridge. It takes on a life of its own. I imagine it dreaming of escape, yanking out its life-line and throwing itself into a creek, to eventually make it downstream to the river and out to sea, only the tip of its white-good iceberg showing as it migrates south for the summer, to the pole, to become stranded in pack ice, happy at last.

If December's run of relatively cool weather was too good to be true, so was the rain. It's drying out again, and I anxiously watch the weather radar for promising signs of life. There is a deluge out to the west, heading this way if it isn't all dumped before tomorrow. Central Queensland is in flood, but here it is only steaming humidity. I want a mushroom life, to stay indoors in dark recesses of the house. It is just too hard to do anything that involves moving from in front of the fan, and the garden suffers.

I'm also covered in an unsightly and insanely itchy rash on my chest, and a million insect bites on my legs following a fruitless search for a Minipeck nest in the seeding head-high grass of our northern neighbour's paddock. Too much sun at the regatta has left my skin raw where I missed with the sunblock, and the seeds have caused an irritation or infection of some sort. Everything putrefies in this heat, including me.

The pearl female went missing about a week ago, and we thought we could hear her calling from down near the neighbour's big dam. I've been keeping tabs on their movements, and it has become suddenly urgent we find her because a contract slasher is coming soon, and there's already been enough dead birds.

I found a pullet on the ground at the mouth of the dome a couple of days ago. She was stiff and hard and ants had already begun their work by the time I gathered her up and buried her in the compost heap. No apparent cause, except that her neck seemed stretched out with its feathers fanned upwards instead of layered down over each other. The Coven didn't seem the slightest bit perturbed by her sudden demise. She was only young, too. I'd found her *lonely as a cloud* at the stock feed place just before Christmas and couldn't bear the thought of her left all by herself, so took her home and put her in with Hen Ali who was in isolation with a sore foot.

They shared the static run, and the sprightly energy of the little one seemed to have a therapeutic effect on the older bird. Gradually Ali became less listless, got herself up, and was showing the nipper how to peck, generally taking on the role of surrogate mother. Before long the pair were inseparable and able to go back in with the Coven — but not without large-scale resistance on the part of the bitches. The pullet had just settled into a middle spot in the pecking order when she mysteriously keeled over.

And then …

Night. Noise downstairs. A flurry of wings against tin.

Shuffling on thongs, we rush down into the dark front yard. A beam of torchlight through chicken wire illuminates the shiny-scaled bulk of a huge carpet snake in the Coop D Ville.

The excited and twittering birds, trying to flatten themselves from a volume to an area against the side of the cage, shrink as far away as possible from the scary monster. A great triangular head, big as my fist, rests on a crossbeam, its coiling body draped heavily over the perches, three feet of tail still outside, caught in the act.

Snakes look wet and slimy but they're not. Their skin is dry and cool, smooth as nail varnish, and I'm in the middle of an Eve moment, standing there amazed, eye to eye with this spectacular creature, evil bad guy of the Western mythos. I'm surprised by its beauty and appalled by its power to load my imagination with meaning. In *Paradise Lost*, Milton describes the serpent spying Eve's approach. Satan is gobsmacked, caught in her headlights and:

> *... abstracted stood*
> *From his own evil, and for the time remained*
> *Stupidly good; of enmity disarmed,*
> *Of guile, of hate, of envy, of revenge ...*

But I reckon it goes both ways. Eve is also struck by the serpent's beauty and she fails to respond to its danger; in a moment it could seize her in its jaws, crush the breath out of her and take all of human history to swallow and digest her. Bad girl. It's her own fault.

I don't know what it is about snakes, apart from the bad biblical wrap. Maybe it's their lack of appendages that makes us recoil. But Eve didn't have any cultural baggage filled with loathing of the serpent, and wasn't at all surprised, apparently, when it spoke to her. And I wouldn't have been either; I am a woman with a talking chicken. As I look into its eye — and it's not often you get to look into the eye of a snake — this one seems to be saying: 'What's your problem? This is my job, leave me alone.'

Had Geoffrey not been here, that is precisely what I would have done. I'd have simply watched, rooted to the spot, as it devoured enough birds to feed its hunger, and then, when it was sluggish and groggy from gutsing itself, I'd have quietly let the remaining birds out, and left the snake in the cage. There is no way I'd have laid a finger on it — that way lies destruction.

But suddenly Geoffrey, with a conscience much more beautiful than mine — he who named the Minipecks — leaps to their defence. He recognises his responsibility to our little captive charges and exercises his duty of care. He'll rid this little kingdom of the dragon.

And defend them he does.

Naked as a newborn, broom in hand, he seizes hold of the snake's enormous tail and tries to drag the beast back out through the tiny opening. But with its bulk, pure muscle and much stronger than his grasp, the snake pulls the rest of itself inside. Geoffrey bashes at the side of the cage and the shiny body drops heavily to the ground where the terrified Minis are freaking out. The serpent, his big bobbing head searching along the wire for an exit, has me transfixed, and all I can think of is to open the door and show it the way out with my torch.

Miraculously, Satan sees his escape and makes his exit:

… not with indented wave,
Prone on the ground, as since; but on his rear,
Circular base of rising folds, that towered
Fold above fold, a surging maze! his head
Crested aloft, and carbuncle his eyes;
With burnished neck of verdant gold, erect
Amidst his circling spires …

and leaves the auditorium. What it lacks in speed, it makes up for in stately grace. It is impossible for a python to be uncool. All fluid, languid movement, it esses its way back into the undergrowth.

But just before daylight, we wake again — to the fluster of wings beating against corrugated iron.

'That's it, it's fucking dead!' There's no stopping Geoffrey.

I gulp back my apprehension at him approaching Satan from the back foot of anger, but he's already down there, again, without so much as a fig leaf between him and his adversary, and I watch the unfolding drama from a safe position on the verandah above.

But this time there is a casualty. The predator must have snuck in before the Minis noticed — and already has one of them in its jaws.

I pull on clothes, grab the torch and scramble downstairs, just as Geoffrey's outrage sends him to that boy-place where heroes rescue maidens and good guys always win. I guess you need to be in a place like that if you're going to face an extremely large reptile wearing nothing but a penis and a pair of thongs.

A scary monster has risen inside him to match his fear of the one he's about to confront, and he seizes his weapon. In the half-moon light, what is actually only a broom I see as a sledgehammer being wielded with super-human strength, smiting at the insinuating body sliding through a rib-crushingly slim space. I can't believe the tenacity of their champion's defence of his little subjects. It is riveting. Surely the cage will be smashed to pieces from the force of his attack — but once again the snake pulls itself into the cage and drops to the ground. At the same time, it drops its prey.

Geoffrey's sledgehammer morphs back into a broom as he sweeps at the poor confounded creature, drags it out of the cage, and again sends it packing. He stoops to pick up the victim's carcass, holds it up in my torchlight and shakes his head — 'Poor Minipeck, I'm sorry' — and sadly tosses it into the bushes, thinking it might satisfy the snake's hunger. But then I remember that they only eat live prey — they are hunters, not bottom feeders. He retrieves the small body, tenderly wraps it in a plastic bag and puts it in the fridge.

We fortify the Coop D Ville against further invasion, screw down all the passable openings and, over dinner, discuss the likelihood of any further trouble. Both of us think the snake seemed smaller the second time, and laugh at how the one that gets away is always much bigger than it really is. Geoffrey needs an early night because he has to get up at dawn tomorrow, to drive forty miles to a job, so we decide to hit the sack early, but before bed he goes out to check on the birds. I thought it unlikely that the snake would return, nursing the headache it had to have after the latest battle, but Geoffrey comes back upstairs with a strange look on his face:

'It's back!'

This time I insist on more sensible attire than bare skin, so he pulls on shorts and a shirt, and a pair of thongs and goes down with the torch. At first he'd thought it was an upright of the cage, but remembering that there isn't one on that side, and noticing this particular upright is also swaying, he's realised that the serpent is looking for a way in.

By the time I'm dressed and downstairs, it is already thinking better of another attack and turning towards the dark protection of the bush. I pick the torch up off the ground and train it on the snake as Geoffrey emerges from under the house with the chook food bin. In shock, I realise what he has in mind. He's going to try to catch it!

He grabs its tail, pulls it away from its escape route and hooks at it with his broom, aiming for the middle, attempting to juggle the snake's looping, roiling body into the bin. Satan, by now not amused, is in self-defence mode, head pulled back in an attitude of strike, all flick-tongued threat, and I'm shitting myself. I know they are not venomous, but the idea of being bitten is just too much.

'Get the lid, quickly.'

It takes a moment for me to realise he is talking to me. On auto-pilot I run for the lid and return to feel myself standing way too close for comfort to a cornered animal with fangs. Somehow, Geoffrey gingerly wrestles it into the bin and slams the lid down, tying it securely with the piece of rope that had been holding up his pants. Only three years in Queensland and already he's become Steve bloody Irwin. If he'd said *Crikey* I'd have either burst into tears or hit him with the broom.

We're sweating, the adrenalin's still pumping, and it doesn't look like sleep will come any time soon, so we sit and share a stubby and talk about sailing model boats, politics, the war — anything we can think of that doesn't involve carpet snakes. After a shower to cool off, and finally fatigued, we fall into bed.

Geoffrey's breathing evens out, and I am floating on the edges of consciousness. Images of great serpent jaws gape at me. That fantastic Renaissance painting of St George with his foot resting on the neck of the dragon, but it's Geoffrey and he's holding up a broom instead of a sword; St Margaret up to her hips in the mouth of a giant snake.

Suddenly it hits me: *This is the way I comprehend the world*. Everything that happens in my life is filtered through a matrix of imagery and metaphor, as if I'm

233

caught in a perpetual dream, but the dreams all belong to the artists whose paintings I've internalised, the authors whose ideas I've made my own.

But what is *my* dream, *my* personal way of seeing?

Am I only a prism?

I've got the room of my own but it doesn't seem to have a clear view. Its window is stained glass, already painted with the visions of others. On the edge of sleep, I search for dreams of my own and an image surfaces, the memory of an old childhood nightmare in which my mosquito net is covered in snakes, seeking out the holes so they can get me, when …

Rustle, rustle. Thump.

Flapping, twittering, terrorised birds.

I'm prepared to leave it in the lap of the gods; there's no way in, after all. But Geoffrey, anticipating a day of working in stifling humidity on no sleep, leaps out of bed in a fury.

'I don't believe this!'

He's reaching for those ludicrous shorts that are now held up only by the force of his will, pulls on boots this time, and storms out. I can hear him cursing and thumping about, and get up to help. He's dragged a big black empty chemical tub down to the cage and is already pulling at the tail of *another* monstrous snake. The previous one *was* smaller — there are two! Geoffrey has its tail, wrenching with all his strength to dislodge it from the side of the cage.

The birds are going to need therapy after this.

He's got the broom and a length of wood, and with one in each hand is trying to chopstick a writhing fifteen-foot-long strand of slithery creature. Clearly, it's never going to happen, the mouth of the tub is too high and the snake too heavy and now it's recovered its balance — if a snake feels such a thing — it is getting aggro.

Satan rears to strike as Geoffrey jumps back, throws the piece of wood across its neck and stands on it, pinning its head down. I am less than useless, only good for aiming the torch beam at its head, anxious that it will be able to reach his ankle. He's actually thought to put on gloves and, to my astonishment, reaches down with one hand and grabs the snake behind its head, releases the pressure of his foot, hefts its considerable weight up and plunges the thing head first into the tub, and with his other hand round its middle plonks it in at the same time and somehow the end of it follows. *Thump*. Both villains are to be consigned to hell.

Finally, we can get some sleep.

Geoffrey breathes softly beside me, the adrenaline hit having eased his usual asthmatic wheeze, but I'm wide awake. The moon has set, and it's just me and myself staring open-eyed into the black density of the night, awash with images and thought. I'd have nights like this in Sydney when I'd been to the theatre, and the play or film had seemed to be specifically about me — starring me, the dramatic arc a reflection of my own life. But tonight's performance was real, no script, no back story, no image to project myself into — just me.

Round and round I chase the meaning of what I've just experienced and try to make sense of it. Why does it keep leading me back to my decision to blow off the teaching gig and isolate myself completely in this Paradise garden of ours?

I'm lying rigid beside the significant other in my world, resisting like crazy the need to toss and turn into a comforting cocoon of bedclothes, so as not to wake him. He wouldn't have to get up and leave our garden to work, if I had taken the teaching job. He already has his hands full running the farm. Bad girl. It's all my fault. I'm so — what, selfish? Lazy?

I'm her, Eve. I'm deep in sin. I've blown off the promise of a solid income and the warm fuzzy goodness of public service. I've ignored the voice of the white angel on my shoulder telling me to do the right thing, in favour of the insinuating little devil on the other, urging me to think only of what's in it for me. I'm a thoughtless, disobedient, delinquent misfit. But then, what's new? I've always been a bad girl. My father's approval meant compromise, my ex-husband's love demanded compromise. I've eaten the apple before and been expelled for it. But this is different. There's no finger-pointing God to blame in my garden. Here, the serpent I have to struggle against is myself.

This time, I've only got myself to blame if I fail. My father counselled his daughter against going to a real art school in favour of a 'proper' career as an art teacher, my husband wanted an obedient fifties housewife. But here in the dark I have no proscribed social role to rail against. I am left to battle alone with the truth about myself and I'm running out of rehearsal time — this is it, my last shot at being who I think I really am.

Christopher and his mum arrive early next morning to find out what all the racket was last night. She couldn't work out if it was us or not. While we were in the midst of our domestic livestock crisis, somewhere in the valley others were embroiled in a domestic. The spaces between people may be greater in the country, but sound travels further in the silence of the night, and every distressed syllable could be heard. Whatever discontent has befallen them, the entire valley now knows it's all *her* fault.

In my St James version of Genesis, the chick and her boyfriend were both there when she ...

took of the fruit thereof, and did eat, and gave also unto her husband with her, and he did eat.

There's nothing there to suggest that he protests, or questions her actions, or is even concerned about her discussing the possibility of eating forbidden fruit with a talking snake. In fact, it's more like he's keeping his trap firmly shut, waiting to see what happens, and when she takes a bite and doesn't die, he tucks in too.

Both sinned, if it is sinful to take a risk. Without the risk there'd be no story, and though the Western myth of creation doesn't hold up for me as a definitive explanation of the origin of the human condition, it's pretty difficult to deny the story's existence. I'm devoted to the symbolism and, I have to admit, trouble in paradise is a fairly persistent metaphor around here.

Wide-eyed, Christopher peers over the lip of the feed bin to stare at the exquisite spiral of reptile coiled in the bottom of it on a bed of wheat. Joanna fiercely holds the lid just a crack open. I peep in too and know there is no way the chooks are going to eat this stuff now that it's drenched in fear-sodden snake piss. They wouldn't go back into the chookhouse for days after I found a snake in the egg boxes. She warns Christopher — 'Look but don't touch' — and I think about Eve's dilemma, and her warning twists around itself in my head as *Listen but don't obey.*

We load the bins onto the tractor and drive over the westen ridge to the bush on the southern perimeter of the property to look for a spot to cast them into damnation for all eternity. Hell, as it turns out, is a pretty good approximation of the paradise from whence the serpents are being evicted. I watch them glide, one after the other, across the open ground away from the scary humans and down into dense scrub. They seemed to have different markings, and slightly different head shapes. But would two males that size share a hunting ground? Perhaps they were mates? They could have been male and female of the same species.

On the drive back I realise our folly. For every action, there is an equal and opposite reaction, and the consequence of removing them will mean an inevitable rise in the rat and mouse population. I do a calculation in my head about the relative cost of a few Minipeck lives compared with the inevitable devastation to my seedlings from mice, which tells me we should have kept one serpent here in paradise, to keep things on an even keel.

11th February

Rainfall last month: Only two and a half inches

Jobs for this month:

- Sow — 9th: Early Purple turnips, beets, carrots, garlic. 19th: Warragul spinach, Rabbit Ear lettuce, kale, Blonde Full Heart endive, dill, pink celery, broccoli. 27th & 28th: cauliflower, snow peas, Purple-Podded peas.
- Plant out tomatoes, capsicums and eggplant.
- Prepare beds for carrots & spring onions, chives & garlic, sow direct.
- Harvest rosellas.
- Re-dig and dress paths — load of woodchip.
- Stove man coming end of the month.
- Lay rat poison.

We never found the nest. I watched from the verandah as the slasher went round and round the paddock in ever diminishing circles, horrified at the thought of Mrs Mini's inability to fight her broodiness and get out of harm's way before the blades dashed her and her eggs to pieces.

There was no hail of feathers and shells — the slasher, trailing a mulcher, reduced everything to confetti and spat it back out onto the cut pasture. The contractor did stop and get out of his cab for a moment to look at something. Perhaps he'd hit a hidden branch or a rock and was only inspecting his blades. I didn't ask. She hasn't returned.

A crow was stealing her eggs. I recall him flying over the house with her not-yet babies in his beak, which makes me reconsider a picture I live with.

From the viewpoint of a god, looking down from above, a child seems to fall backwards and splash down into the warm-grey chop on a turbulent lake of thickly brushed oil paint. But does it? The body of the mother, turgid, pink and congested, refracts beneath the surface, with only her face and hand above it, in the same plane as her baby-blue child. It is impossible to decide whether the child is falling into her embrace, or being violently expelled from the lake.

Their heads are crowned by a murder of crows swooping at the child, descending in front of the mother's brow, separating the figures in space. Her body is heavy under the surface of the picture; she can only free one hand to save the baby. Too late — one crow is already pecking at an eye, the other bores into an ear, maiming her perfect creation who is adrift now, already disconnected from her. She wears a mask of serenity, but every stroke of the brush on her face betrays her agitation at her incapacity to save her baby. His blue body (the reason I imagine him a boy) wants to recede, but his mother's submerged red-hued hips keep him afloat.

But those crows could also be a crown of thorns, if he's the Christ child, which he is in my imagination. The Madonna and Child has been a persistent template for the past several thousand years — all the big-time pagan gods since Horus have had a virgin for a mother. So, when you make that connection, the most extraordinary thing happens; the image time-shifts 33 years in a moment, and becomes Pieta — the image of the Virgin nursing the crucified Christ. The blue baby is suddenly a corpse lying in his mother's lap, and her face shape-shifts into a mask of grief as her son becomes carion to crows.

This painting is by my first mentor, Davida Allen. Rose Creswell taught me how to read, Davida taught me how to see. She was my painting teacher, and introduced me to my son's father, her dealer, who took up my education where she left off. I babysat her daughters, and she taught me how to be a mother. She is Evan's god-mother, and I am fortunate to have this work by her hand. In it is encoded a deep, deep mystery — Western women's business. By continually tying to fathom its depths of meaning, I find myself situated firmly between birth and death. The source and the embodiment of both.

However, Mrs Mini's crow has got his karma: his glossy blue-black body was found lying near the base of one of Geoffrey's trees, sleek and fat, dead as a dodo. High-cholesterol diet equals heart attack.

It's not all doom and gloom, though. Number One is a mother, no longer the carefree gadabout. She dropped her calf early last month, a heifer, the first for the new year, and the very image of her dam. I suppose that makes us grandparents. We went to the top of the ridge to walk the fence line and check for breaks, and there she was, spindle-legged and wobbly, peeping at us between her mother's legs. The white blaze on Number One's forehead and the placement of her stubby horns — she is the only one in the herd to have them — gives this new mum a constant look of dismay, as if to say, 'I was born for better things than this, I could be in movies, get me out of here!' And she has her very own recognisable moo to match her expression, a high-pitched imploring *noooooo.*

I can hear her now, every so often, between gaps in the music we're playing. It's been a long, hot day that has finally just cooled down into evening, so we're out on the verandah watching the full moon rise over a beer or three. An hour later she's still at it. Helen's Excalibur story comes to mind and I'm starting to worry something might be wrong.

By now the moon is high and there's plenty of light to see by, so we set out to find her. It's a hike. The cows are in the top paddock, because the slasher has been in the mango paddock and there's no feed for them there. The night is mild and I'm surprised by the clarity of the light and the difference the slashed grass makes; a giant golf course, just not flat. The moon accompanies us, her reflection keeping pace over the surface of the dam as we make our way to the yards. She cuts crisp shadows around us, throwing them into our path. We walk through the bowl of space as if inside a crystal ball, and my head fills with the yeasty perfume of newly mown grass.

We follow our ears towards the mournful moan of Number One. And there she is on one side of a fence, and her calf on the other, too confused by her mother's carry-on to move. Geoffrey opens the gate for Number One to join the rest of the herd and looks around for the broken strands of fencing she must have pushed through to get herself into such a predicament. I stand there unable to move, charmed by the sight of the herd grazing, swimming in a silver sea of tranquillity. The only sound is the swish of their tongues sweeping up grass, punctuated by a sharp squeak as they yank it free.

We take the long way back past the big pine trees on the eastern ridge and sit for a moment to take in the view out to sea. What a piece of luck to find myself here, where every beauty seems the same as every other, every day. If I really did believe in karma, I could only wonder what magnanimous, selfless acts of charity and goodness I must have committed in a previous life to have deserved a go at heaven on earth. I look out across the valleys below dotted with the lights of houses, and follow the intermittent passage of headlights along the highway, and wonder what my next step will be on the road between birth and death. It couldn't get any better than this, surely?

It's shaping up to be the same as last year, relentlessly hot. I've already given lettuce a miss and have decided just to go for tomatoes, corn, melons, capsicum and eggplant. Even basil fades in this heat. The garden is gasping and thirsty after a hot, dry January. I'm back to manning the pump and bucketing water to the citrus. But I make a mortifying mistake.

Rather than pump up from the dwindling dam, or dip from the sludge-filled tub by the seed house, I'm determined to give my thirsty little seedlings a vital start. We've been frugal with water all summer because of the scarcity of good rain, so it feels reasonable to risk a couple of dozen gallons of fresh clean water up to the garden.

But I forget to turn it off.

I got sidetracked; fed and watered the Coven and the Minis, watered the citrus, did the washing-up, weeded the front gardens, updated my diaries and planting schedule, did a stretch on the Internet reading the news, and a dozen other things … Five hours later, I am horrified. Geoffrey tries to console me, says it will only amount to about six inches' loss from the tank, but still, lesson learned.

Never, never, never leave the hose running and walk away.

As penance, I drive to the other side of town to collect a load of woodchip to re-cover the rotted, overgrown garden paths, and spend the next day digging the old stuff out and onto garden beds. I lay newspaper in the remaining furrow and pile the new chips into it, a barrowload at a time. It takes an entire afternoon of appropriately punishing physical labour. It would probably take a twenty-one-year-old bloke only a couple of hours, but I am a middle-aged woman with a dodgy disc and a guilty conscience, and need to stop for swigs of cold water and a breather every twenty minutes. The result is profoundly pleasing — beautiful tan bark passageways circling the green anarchy of the beds, with a clear view of any dodgy wildlife that may be lurking at my feet.

I may be unemployed at the moment, but I'm by no means under-employed. Every day that I open my eyes, an endless array of tasks stretches out in all directions. I won't get any paid work till second term, when teachers start to feel the strain, when all their good intentions and hopeful enthusiasm gets ground down by the reality of what they are trying to do. In second term they start to take a day here and there to get over the first cold of the year. They don't fully recover because of the responsibility they feel, and with each subsequent bout of illness it takes them longer and longer to get out of bed. By term three they've had it, and the army of supply teachers is called in to stop the emotional and physical leaks. I'm only mildly discomforted now by my decision to forgo full-time work. Something will turn up eventually. It always does.

Till then, I'll be busy finding ways to avoid spending money. I don't know where people get off suggesting that the unemployed are lazy. Where on earth do they get the idea that being penniless equals a life of aimless ease? Not having cash means doing everything myself. I follow Geoffrey's slasher, rake and collect the cut grass, pile it into a big plastic mattress bag and drag it home to mulch the garden. We limit trips in the car to a couple of times a week because the cost of petrol is so punishing, I mend tatty clothes, dubbin my boots to preserve the leather, bottle fruit for winter, reuse the backs of sheets of paper, save slivers of soap and cut open toothpaste tubes.

This is the cost of keeping my heirlooms. I know I could sell a picture if we ever get really desperate, but pictures are for keeping, not selling — unless you are the artist or their dealer. To sell my collection would be like selling my soul. It is the diary of who I am, and no amount of money could compensate their absence from my life.

Geoffrey has had work off the farm. Not much, just a couple of days here and there. Being a man with a set of hands accustomed to prodigious use, and after so long with barely any contact with the outside world, he tells me he is eager for it. But if it wasn't for the fact that he maintains his art benefits from his forays out into the world of work and contact with other human beings, the sum doesn't add up. By the time fuel, tax, wear and tear on tools and the car are deducted, there's bugger-all left over for the price of a few beers. He arrives home utterly shagged, and is asleep by 7 pm, so he can get up and do it all over again the next day.

Teaching may be gruelling, on an emotional and intellectual plane, but his work is physical and dangerous. Too much sun and not enough hydration on a building site, with power tools and electricity and heights — it's a trip to the hospital, or worse, just waiting to happen. And forget insurance — there's no way that falls inside our budget. Our only insurance is care. I prefer him to take his personal risks where I can see him, or at least hear the whistle I insist he wears when he heads off up the hill on the tractor. Especially now that it's raining. Pissing down. My back-breaking, bark-shovelling penance has paid off.

Three days of constant, plummeting, drowning rain. It's going to be okay, the tank is replenished of the six inches I squandered in one drop. The new planting is loving it, and the overflow is running again. When the rain lets up enough to see through, we go outside, Geoffrey in his bright, safety-orange wet-weather jacket inherited from his sailing career — a heavy-duty, rounding-the-horn kind of raincoat — and me in my tragic, primary-school-yellow plastic job, patched up with sticky-back adhesive, and completely ineffective in these conditions. He's dry by the end of our walk, and I'm drenched, mostly from taking childish delight in splashing about in the pools of water that lay in potholes along the road. The entire landscape looks as if it has been steam-cleaned, which, if you think about it, it has.

The rain has come at just the right time for my rosella crop. Rosellas are a variety of hibiscus. I planted them in spring as a test for a cash crop. They seem to do okay here, have no pests and no problems with rot. They are extremely hardy — my idea of the perfect plant, really: looks after itself. They flower in delicate, yellow, red-centred blooms that wither to pink in one day. The bloom springs directly from bright red stems along with long, slender blue-green leaves. The calyx of the flower is the edible part, bright red and tangy-citrus flavoured. Excellent for jam, syrups, even as a cabbage substitute, and they have many medicinal uses. I dedicated three front beds to them to see what density they can be planted to, and whether I need to water them or not; and the first test bed is now bearing like crazy.

I've been pulling bucketloads of flower pods off nine plants for the last week — trouble is, harvesting is extremely labour intensive, as is shucking the seed from the fruit. This will probably explain why no one seems to grow them and why there is a niche market. Added to this minor setback, mine have a natural defender — the jumping ant. If I wish to harvest, I have to dress up as securely as a beekeeper, because jumping ants are extremely territorial, and their sting is ferocious. There will be a few bottles of jam and chutney this year, but no vast projected income.

And still it is raining — weeks of leaden skies and overnight drizzle, much more like the kind of falls we should get at this time of the year. But rain in this volume is not without its downside. All the tomatoes and bananas have split their skins from the sudden increase in moisture, and the dome is a quagmire. The farm ute is not 4WD and the wheels spin at the bottom of the driveway if backed too far onto wet grass. There is nothing more femininely depressing than the knowledge that I'll have to get Geoffrey to drive it out with my weight in the back holding it down. It doesn't work the other way round.

Worst of all, the wildlife thinks that anywhere dry is a perfectly good place to seek shelter, including in the house. A little blue-tongued lizard claimed squatter's rights. I thought I'd seen something out of the corner of my eye for a few days, scuttling between Geoffrey's sail loft and the bathroom, and when we finally bailed it up, it got bolshy about its eviction. The buggers bite!

But it's the lace monitor that gets to me. If I leave the kitchen screen door open just once, there he is, in all his Victorian doily splendour, thinking he can just cruise on in and drape himself over a table or something. I'm tuned in now, after three years. I'll be engaged in something thought-absorbing, then get this *what's going on in the kitchen* sensation, and there, shoulders over the doorstep, is the intruder. And every time it happens, I shout and clap my hands so hard I bruise my fingers — and it's off, across the verandah's high side, launching itself over a ten-foot drop. That's got to hurt. I can't imagine why it keeps it up. Reptile brain, I guess.

Sookachook does her best to keep me informed of territorial incursions, but she's got Sookatoo to contend with now, which is obviously diverting her attention. Sookatoo is one of four clapped-out old layers I purchased from a free-range egg producer. Unlike her sisters, who keeled over from the shock of not being under extreme and constant stress, she did all right for a few months, but then came down with Sookachook's ailment — no leg action. Hers is much worse; her right leg is totally frozen, and drags out behind her — no chance of standing or walking, so she's joined her ungracious companion on the front verandah. Now there are two foam boxes in the ward. And in the spirit of democracy (actually, Sookachook's bad-tempered insistence on equality), I've had to provide equivalent dining arrangements. They have matching bowls, water containers and bedding. It's better that way.

But miraculously, following the admission of Sookatoo, Sookachook's health has improved. Suddenly, she can walk. I have my suspicions about the sneakiness of chickens when it comes to cashing in on free health care, but really, it's probably got more to do with power and the pecking order of two. Sookachook is up on her pins and crapping all over the verandah, about to be renamed Poopachook or banished to the horror of the dome if she's not careful.

I seem to be wallowing in it at the moment. The smell of dung clings to everything in this wet. Even my clothes get covered in it when we get up close to the cows. It's time to cut out the weaners; two little bulls need to be castrated and Panda's beautiful black calf is going to market. I tell myself that because she is so sleek and placid someone will buy her for a herd, but we'll have no control over her fate once she's on the beef bus.

It's a lot easier to handle them since we poured a slab of concrete under the crush. Now they don't slip in the slush of mud and manure underfoot. The crush needed to be pulled apart, repaired and kill-rusted anyway, so we took the opportunity to fix the problem, with Liz — who, like me, thinks getting filthy and mucking in on the boy jobs is a form of fun. It took three of us most of the morning to complete the task; Geoffrey did the formwork while we girls set up the mixer.

The tractor has a generator attachment that can produce 240 volts to run the machine, and once the mixer was going we started feeding the ingredients into its gob to make the mud. Nothing to it — just like making a cake, except that sand and cement and gravel are a little bit more difficult to manipulate than a cup or two of flour. I can't believe how many loads that hole swallowed before it was ready to float. That is my favourite part, patting the concrete down into the raised reo, then floating a flat piece of wood over the gluggy surface to level it to that shiny steel finish. Unfortunately, what was called for was a rough foothold for the cattle, so my perfect surface had to be deeply scored once it was set hard enough.

A slab is a beautiful thing, solidified water, and I love to watch the process. I've observed the pouring of several, so consider myself a bit of a connoisseur. One craftsman who came to lay a new slab under our house turned up with two strapping sons and one enormous bitch. The dog guarded the tools in the back of the truck, the boys did all the heavy work, and he pretty much just supervised. And chatted.

We got to talking about his dog, a mountainous slobber-jawed thing about as big as me. I was impressed by the placidity of such a confronting-looking creature. He laughed: 'Yeah, she is now, but you oughta see 'er when she goes off.'

I was burning to know what he meant by 'go off'.

'Huntin' dog.'

'Oh yeah?' My intonation urged him to elaborate.

'Pigs.'

'She's a pig dog?' She didn't look much like a bull terrier to me.

'Well, she'll have a go at anything, but,' he nodded in the direction of the two young gods shovelling wet concrete, 'we hunt feral pigs.' By now I was totally hooked and needed to know the details. My head was full of images of blokes on trucks with spotlights and guns, bashing through the bush, and I told him about the big pig shoots up north that would end in beery festivals of the flesh.

He grinned: 'Nah, guns are for sooks, we're knife men.'

He told me how they hunt. The dogs do all the work. They find the quarry and, when it's cornered, worry at it and wear it down. I looked at the old bitch licking my hand and noticed the scars and tattered ears and realised that her big wet pink tongue was barred by a row of yellow teeth set in a jaw that could lock onto the throat of a pig. She'd risk being gored by tusks at the shoulder, gut and haunch when her master commanded it. At the final moment, he would call off the dogs, plunge his knife into the pig's jugular and finish the job.

'You make sure you don't miss.'

I now looked like a total idiot, with my mouth agape. I was stroking the drooling jowls of a killing machine, while in conversation with a man who could leap onto the back of an enraged beast and kill it. He had a glint in his eye and had maybe embroidered his story to make my eyes pop completely out of my head — but I still can't believe that such apparently ordinary guys can spend all week at their back-breaking job, and then go out on the weekends to risk their lives in a primal struggle with a wild beast.

All I could manage in response was, 'Do you reckon she'd go a feral cat?'

What makes some people (and it's not just blokes) want to do that? I can take the head off a chicken, but it's not sport. It fills me with pity to take an animal's life. I don't lose sleep over it, but I don't take it lightly, and I certainly don't get excited by the prospect of it. I suppose the culling of feral animals can be justified, but I find it completely incomprehensible to attach any joy to the act.

I have the same problem with the masters of war who set their dogs on the hunt. Except they don't have the guts to do the deed themselves. They just leave it to the dogs to savage their quarry, and watch the carnage on TV. I might be able to convince myself that my involvement in the war is out of my hands, that it's a long way away and not really anything to do with me personally, and anyway, the economy is going gangbusters and I've got a lifestyle to get on with; I might eventually be able to push the almost half a million innocent deaths out of my thoughts, if it wasn't for the fact that my nephew has just joined the army.

He's fallen for the advertising campaign, and has lined up like an obedient puppy for a pat on the head from old men who praise his bravery and virtue and call him a hero. But I doubt he's read the fine print of the contract. It probably hasn't entered his snowy slouch-hatted head that he may have to kill people, or might end up in a body bag himself, with a tag on his toe that reads, *Your war is over, you can come home forever.*

Or maybe he has — maybe he's so bored by the inevitable prospect of a mortgage and three kids by the time he's twenty-five, that he'd rather take the risk; and besides, at his age, he's immortal anyway: a young god, and if he keeps his spit-and-polished boots on, he'll never leave his heel exposed.

But there is nothing to be done about it. He is not my son. He is an adult. It is his life, if he's lucky enough to hang onto it. Still, the news is coloured differently now. What was once an intellectual abstraction has become personal. Now I grind my teeth in seething rage when I hear the rhetorical sludge that pours out of my radio, and am delighted by the prospect that the willing coalition has its tail between its legs. I don't want my sister's child sacrificed to a lie. If that makes me a traitor, shoot me.

I'm not alone, though. There are all types of subversives out here in the back blocks: New-Age philosophers, secessionists, anti-Semites, Hanson loyalists, end-of-days God-botherers, people who refuse to shop at Woolworths, anti-development lobbyists, Christians for social justice, anti-war protesters, greenies, and conspiracy theorists of every possible persuasion. I know this because most of them write letters to the editor of the local magazine, which I proofread at mate's rates each month. To her credit, she publishes them all without fear or favour. They range from sane and well informed to completely loony. The magazine makes for interesting and amusing reading — and to date I've not seen one single lifestyle article between its covers. It's the only free press around these parts, since Murdoch bought up everything else about two and a half seconds after the new cross-media laws were passed. And I never know when I'm going to run into one of her correspondents.

A local bloke came to the house to clean our chimney and repair the seal on the fireplace. We didn't realise the broken seal was so bad that for two years it's been the reason we've had to feed the fire twice as much fuel as it should need. This explains why logs burned out in the wee hours, leaving the house freezing in the mornings. He took a look at the new cooker too, to make sure it would be safely serviceable. The only thing left to do now is plumb it in before winter: its new home is finished and whenever I enter the room I feel like I'm in the middle of a Chardin still life; the tall copper chimney, framed by a sap-green wall, reflects all my pretty orange enamel pots and pans hanging there on brass hooks.

As he put the finishing touches to the stove door I asked him about the glass in it, and what temperature it could withstand when, out of the blue, like a schoolboy with a dirty secret he took me into his confidence and told me about a website that would reveal a whole lot of information about the melting point — nudge-nudge — of structural steel — wink-wink. Somehow he'd steered the subject round to 9/11 and his own complex conspiracy theory on the matter.

He didn't even know I become irrationally incensed every time an American expert gets airplay on my-ABC and uses the term *we*, as if speaking on my behalf. I wondered if he got round to this issue with all the middle-aged women in the area, or just old lefties like me.

When he'd gone, I related the whole strange conversation to Geoffrey, who just grinned and pointed to the fridge. Stove-guy must have glanced at it on his way through the living room and seen the little magnetic whiteboard headed:

Things to do today.

I had jokingly written on it that old anarchist graffiti line:

Smash the State.

Among the notes, phone numbers, postcards and clippings plastered to the fridge, that is the one thing that he saw, enough to give him permission to risk exposure. What would our conversation have been about had it not been there? The weather, no doubt.

It's still raining; sticky and slippery underfoot, wet leaf matter and mud trailing through the kitchen to the phone and the bathroom. Thank goodness I'm not a neat-freak or I'd need a shrink by now. I suspect that my mother casts a mortified eye over my kitchen floor every time she visits. But there's just no point to cleaning floors here. Red clay is either falling out of the thick tread of boots in wet weather, or finds its way in as clouds of dust from the dirt road in the dry. Besides, where's the pleasure in cleaning unless you can see where you've been?

Then there's Sookachook. Since recently being banished from the verandah, she's developed an irresistible need to come into the kitchen to pick over the crumbs and debris. If she was a little more careful with her backside, I don't think I'd mind, but so far, it has proven impossible to toilet train a chicken. I chase her out yet again, and slam the screen door on her ludicrously comical, slipping and sliding retreat. But she has reminded me why I'm here in the kitchen in the first place. I need an egg.

A dribble of golden yolk, a little rainwater, and a dob of translucent iron oxide — I'm trying to get the consistency of a glaze right, so it will dry evenly. If not, cockroaches will suck it off overnight, right down to the chalky ground. Egg tempera may look like paint, but it's a midnight feast to the critters that have moved into the studio now that I'm painting again.

I'm back at the beginning, back to basics, working on an art-school exercise in form in volume. It's a still life, but I'm the only one who knows that. A few slabs of pale sienna laid up against some darker patches of umber don't resemble anything much. It's going to be a bowl of eggs, but at the moment it's a bit of a mess. I've got the under-painting right, but the energy of the initial drawing is getting lost in the process of building up the form of the pale globes. They look more like a chook's breakfast than eggs.

I can't believe how difficult this little painting has become. I thought that limiting its palette would make things easier to handle, but it isn't — the image is turning into mud in my hands. The only thing to do is stop for a moment, pull my focus back from the surface, go back to the original drawing and try to work out how to fix it.

I'm sorely tempted to go and make a coffee or fire up the computer and fool around on the Web, anything other than face up to the problem. There's certainly a floor that could be swept, or a curtain to iron, but even the Coven will have to wait this afternoon. I'm busy. I'm working. Or rather, wrestling with myself, playing games in my head, inventing little rewards to keep myself in the studio: if I stay and resolve this, I can have a cigarette. I seal the deal with myself by lighting up.

A rising eddy of blue-tinged smoke, fragrant as incense, curls at my fingertips. It swirls and plumes like ink in water. Like my paint, physical and fugitive as a puff of smoke. Which is really all it is — just powdered pigment in suspension, to catch light, hold it still, and imprison it in minute, carefully arranged prisms of colour-dust.

Blue! That's it! The shadows need to be blue! And with the film of oxide over them — well, the oxide will warm up the gleaming ground beneath the eggs, and they'll jump forward. Brilliant! Maybe. There's only one way to find out.

By the time I've laid down the new shadows and applied the glaze, my reward has burnt down to a two-inch calcined grub of ash. I never smoke as much when I need two hands for what I'm doing. Still, I must remember to make rollies in future — they don't burn away, they just go out. It's for the pause as much as my addiction, a meditation to bring things back to mind, rather than being caught in a stream of activity. Rolling a cigarette is contemplative — all slow, repetitive movements: snugging the moist wad of tobacco into its paper, sealing it with a lick and a twist between fingertips. As contemplative as cleaning up.

The cleaning of brushes is absolutely necessary. They need as much care as hair to retain their silken softness, but leaving enough tooth on the bristles to pick up the paint. I don't have a big collection of quality brushes, so I need to be methodical about cleaning them, especially favourites, the ones that make just the right mark in just the right way. It's these little things, these rituals, that I'm rediscovering. The painting part is just plain soul-destroying so far. I'm so rusty, I can barely cope with mixing the most rudimentary tertiary tint, but the studio rituals are reasserting their pull on my attention, drawing me back into the practice.

That's all it requires — practice. A little hand-eye coordination, and the obsessive dedication to want to spend every spare moment glued to the object of my imagination. But this time, no distractions, no deviations. This time, life won't get in the way.

I know all of this is much easier said than done, but it is the *doing* that counts. All the intention in the world is irrelevant without action. Then, in the midst of activity, time dissolves into the present moment, hours evaporate, and the white silence of concentration rings in my ears, high-pitched and vibrant as cicada song. Or perhaps it is the song of myself, inside my own energy field. Whatever it is, I now find myself longing for that sound, and know how to get it started — the sharp crack of eggshell. Once an egg is open, I have the imperative to use it — it won't keep, and the Coven has gone to a lot of trouble to produce such miraculous things for my amusement.

Occasionally, while out weeding or watering seedlings, I catch one of the girls at the moment of lay. Burridge, sitting there in her chooky, nesting posture, all fluffed up in the laying box, carefully drapes bits of loose chaff across her back; then she slowly rises, head pulled into her neck feathers, and stands there motionless, with a strange faraway look in her eye. If they are within sight, the others will adopt the same pose: stand still and wait outside the mouth of the box. It takes some time — then *thud*, the egg falls — but Burridge remains standing, suspended in the zone, dazed, out there in the place females go to when they give birth. It never fails to make me cringe — *ouch*, that has got to hurt.

She seems to be in shock, stunned, till somebody outside breaks the spell by pecking at her, or dragging her off the nest by her comb because she's causing a log jam, and she busts out of there in a flurry, *buckarking* at the top of her voice. It'd be criminal to waste such a hard-won gift as that. And now that Fluffy is on the job, I know that they are potential baby chickens, too. Every egg I break over a picture, or breakfast, is a thwarted potential life, so I feel compelled to do the best I can with it.

From downstairs, I hear the sharp electrical crack of a jack being plugged into an amp. Geoffrey is back in his studio too, about to record a guitar track on a new song. Perhaps it's the cooler weather, or the rain that keeps him from farm tasks, but the onset of autumn always seems to find him musically productive.

This new song is a joint effort, about the physics of a kiss and how:

It expands you like a universe till you could fly apart,
but the strong force holds your matter back,
pulling particles to pieces.

Pollen out of stamen, out of flower,
out of stem and leaf, from gut and gland,
corpuscle and vein, through rushing heart.

In cell sac, colliding, uncurl and split,
battalions of becoming,
awaiting the fatal embrace of each other.

As he plays, I hear my own voice rise up through the floorboards on a wave of his blue guitar. And I think it is beautiful.

Autumn

12th March

Rainfall last month: Eight and a half glorious, soggy inches!

Jobs for this month:

- Sow — 9th & 10th: beets, carrots, leeks.
  22nd & 23rd: Lazy Wife beans, Romanesco broccoli, basil, Bok Choy cabbage, celery, Bunyards Matchless, Lollo Biondo lettuce, parsley, Rainbow Chard silverbeet.
  27th: Black Krim tomato, eggplant, capsicum, Kipfler potatoes.
- Clear old carrot bed & plant climbing beans.
- Move chooks onto last two beds in back garden — out at the end of the month.
- Prune peach tree hard.
- Repair static chook run fence.
- Where is Mrs Mini 3? Find her nest.

It is still raining intermittently, and dense violet cloud promises more. The valley is lovely when it is like this: overcast, dripping, and the humidity bearable. My morning spider's web is almost perfect, strung with a spangle of liquid rainbow gems. Whipbirds slice and crack the sparkling air. I nip out in my new raincoat with an armful of mulch to cover the sludge in the Coven's dome. Geoffrey pulls on his boots.

We're going to the top of the western ridge to open a gate for the cows and check on the progress of a new week-old heifer. I also want to see how lovely Number Eight is going. She's the prettiest little cow in the herd, with her perpetually worried look. She is pregnant, but I can't imagine how she's going to fit a whole calf inside her small, dainty frame. She still remembers me from her own calfhood, and never fails to sniff my outstretched hand in the hope of oranges.

We take the path along the northern fence line that leads up beside the edge of a stand of box. The track is heavy-going, greasy and covered in slippery rotting leaf matter. There are long skid marks from the crest of the hill, where cows have lost their footing and tobogganed down. At any moment I might do the same in my old tread-worn wellies.

At the top of the ridge I stop to suck in the cool moist air, peel the steamy plastic from my clammy skin, and take in the early morning view. A fairy floss of mist rises wispy as Grandpa's beard from the hollows of the valley below, and glassy pasture glimmers in the new day's sunlight now streaming through a break in the cloud cover. The plantation's flushed new growth quivers in the rising breeze, and I am struck dumb. It's not just that I can barely breathe from the climb, it's that the valley is completely gorgeous from up here. I make a mental note to add 'Give up smoking' to my list of jobs for next month. I never want to be prevented from making this climb.

The only thing to break the silence, apart from the pounding thump of blood at my temples, is the joyous *squeegwaw* of the Minipecks. I can't believe I can hear them all the way up here. The youngsters are starting to show their sex traits, a large part of which is their voice. The sexes have different calls, and their fathers have taken to taunting the young males through the cage, which gets them all going at once. The display is amusing to watch, but makes it almost impossible to hear anything. They only do it in the morning and evening, but what a racket! When they all go off at once the raucous calling sounds like an un-oiled machine about to fly apart. Even though the studio is supposed to be soundproof, they can still be heard faintly in recordings and so are banished to the farthest end of the yard, out of microphone range.

Just as well they are not cats or they'd be down a life. A few days ago, we didn't register a strange bump in the night above the heavy rain, and woke next morning to find two trees that had been growing in the gully had fallen, missing the Coop D Ville by only inches. It took the rest of the morning to chainsaw through the mess of tangled liana, giant strangling things that bleed bright red when cut, and clear a path through to the cage.

The trail of devastation that follows the Coop round the garden is getting a bit much, too. They've turned the yard into a cesspit, and are now eating their body weight in grain, most of which they spill. When the Coop moves, the residue feeds the now fat and sleek bush turkey population. Time to think about culling.

Much as I love the idea of autumn, I feel myself falling like the frangipani leaves. Not into depression, though it may look like that from the outside as I withdraw and become silent in preparation for the coming shorter days and less light.

This morning I woke up weeping from a dream about my last day at work. I'd spent all day doing millions of stupid approach–avoidance tasks, till it came to the moment when I had to say goodbye for the last time to Rose. She's my last mentor, I don't think I'll need another one. And besides, Therese has informally appointed me hers. I feel deeply indebted to Rose for her generosity and friendship. She gave me a job and rescued me during my divorce, and showed me it was possible to invent a new way to be in the world.

I'm left with the lingering image of us locked in a howling embrace. The emotion of it is so strong, tears well up when I think about it — guess I'm not really over the loss of that previous life yet. I still miss Rose to bits. I miss the laughter, the shared exhilaration of finding genius in the slush pile, hundreds of drinks after work, and saving the world: I really miss saving the world with Rose. And I miss the coven — the human one.

The last time I saw Hen Jane's namesake was at her kitchen table — a night we'd shed tears about the world, how weird it's all gone, how we'd failed to stop the rot on our watch. And visiting since then, over lunch at the Bayswater, out of the intimate loop of knowingness and familiarity with my girlfriends, I've found myself disconnected and unable to speak. The telephone feels worse than useless for making sense of the empty mess of space between utterances — without creases at the edges of eyes or the quick arch of an eyebrow for clues. Relationship, belonging; you can't take it with you.

I'm not lonely, I don't pine for it, I just remember the way it used to be, and how I felt fondly hugged by those other lives, part of a mutual experience. But now I'm held by other arms, to the redolent bosom of family.

My parents celebrated their fiftieth wedding anniversary this month. Imagine, fifty years with the same person. It used to be something people aspired to, now it is a marvel. I actually managed to be a good girl, even though close proximity to my father usually results in a blue. We've argued for as long as I can remember, mostly about politics and society. It started as a childish way to get all his attention, then grew into our relationship. And old habits die hard. It takes all my concentration not to bite on his bait, to shut up, and just let him be right, because now I know how much our lifelong conflict makes my mother's heart hurt.

I made the point in my eldest-child speech that my father's recognition of her lovely soul was his greatest claim to fame. He saw her beauty, and that is all he's ever really needed to know. Their children the icing on the wedding cake; their grandchildren are so many flowers tied up in ribbons, bows and love knots. No argument there.

Aunties I'd not seen for years came up to me with photographs of their progeny — the grandchildren of my cousins, and explained in minute detail, which I was sure to forget instantly, the names, relationships, likenesses. 'He's just like his mother' — a woman I'd never be likely to meet in the course of our far-flung lives. I didn't get it at the time, their need to tell me who was who, but on the drive home, Geoffrey pointed out that I am now an elder of the clan. It is my job to recognise the next generation. I share responsibility for them. It never occurred to me to take along a photograph of my own son to pass round. Perhaps I only have to make sure my sisters recognise our family face in Evan's children.

Evan's six-year-old face stares down at me from his portrait on the wall. He wears a too-serious blazer with gold buttons, scuffed school shoes, and a tie at the collar of his blue school shirt, and sits uncomfortably in a too-large chair, floating, hanging on for dear life to its arms, a lost boy adrift in a too-big world. The painting is by Lewis Miller, a Melbourne painter who, by the craft and deft touch of this portrait of my child, deserves every bit of his acclaim. Each smear of paint builds the unmistakable form of the adult face that Lewis somehow detected beneath the chubba-bubba plumpness of Evan's childish pout.

Apart from those elements there's a hat, his father's Borsalino, resting on the floor to his left, and on the other side, a pet tortoise. By association, it looks like one of those sideshow tricks — which shell is the pea under? His feet rest on a densely painted persian rug. And all the movement, suggested by an arrow shape of grey cement floor, rushes towards the edge of the frame, as if the carpet is about to magically take flight and carry him with it. The expression on his face is forlorn; reluctant, worried.

Now he is out there, beyond the frame of childhood, beyond my influence. He is a man, in command of himself, about to graduate from university, move to London to work and, he declares, never come home again. I don't believe him, though.

He came, he ate, he slept.

On his last visit here, while he slept I made compost, which he thinks is revolting. It took a few days for his carefully constructed and maintained facade to crumble enough for me to glimpse the little prince he's imprisoned in his castle wall. Eventually he relaxed and became himself — the boy I recognise.

Geoffrey took him sailing. The sight of two grown men in a small dinghy was a worry. There, in the time warp of my sacred site, down on the riverbank at Munna Point, I watched anxiously from the shore. They made it back without capsizing, and Evan hasn't shut up about it since.

He emailed today, but I find it difficult to write back with any news that he'd be vaguely interested in. The farm has its own momentum and we fit in with it, loaded up with daily duties by a force much larger than us. And I certainly don't mention my tentative re-entry into my studio. That information is strictly on a need-to-know basis. I've barely admitted it to myself.

The rain has stopped, and now I'm afraid of an extended long dry winter if April fails to deliver its wet. There is a lull in garden production till the first backyard beds mature. Having let the front beds go to weed, my pickings from the vegetable garden presently are slim, and I occasionally find myself in town reluctantly purchasing broccoli and lettuce. Most of the produce that is coming on now has nothing to do with my puny efforts: fig, guava, bananas, ice-cream bean, chocolate sapote, tamarillo, wild passionfruit and self-seeded bell-lantern peppers — all are bearing prolifically. With such abundance of tropical exotics, it's difficult to project my thoughts into the coming cold weather — broad beans, snow peas, caulies, and a fire at night.

And who'd have thought there could be such a thing as too much rain? The garden beds show patches where the clay is still too dense and drainage is a problem. I've made drawings so I know where to dig in more grass clippings and manure next time the Coven goes round.

Will I ever master this gardening thing? So many variables, so much time and energy spent thinking it into being. Still so much to learn.

A grey goshawk alights in a tree that instantaneously explodes with every other bird that was in it. Now, that's a tree change! They aren't rare. My field guide says they're 'locally common, but generally scarce'. I've only ever seen this one, though it must have a mate somewhere. They are about as big as a sulphur-crested cockatoo, and it's not till you see the reaction of other species that you realise it's a bird of prey.

Something has sent the Minipecks into a frenzy. I go out to investigate the frantic shrieking from the top of the high dam wall — perhaps I'll find their nest! But their voices lead me to the last Mrs Mini. Too late.

On the way back to the house, as I struggle to close the three-strand-tangle of barbed-wire gate, I find her, stiff and cold in the dewy grass at my feet. I must have walked right past her. I pick her up and try to work out what has killed her — she doesn't seem to have any puncture marks on her body, but I can't be sure till I pluck her. We won't eat it but if the carcass is okay I'll cook it for the Coven; if not, it'll go into the compost.

Back at the house I lay her on the verandah while I put a pot of water on, to scald her feathers off, and then the damnedest thing happens. I watch through the window as her husbands approach — she had three, being the last female standing. They never come onto the verandah, but now they are filing up the two steps, one after the other, and tentatively edging closer to the body of their ex-mate. Bowing their heads up and down, they process in a circle round her corpse. It is as if they are as confused and perplexed by her death as I am, and can't understand where she is now; though her body is there, she isn't. And it looks for all the world like the Minipecks are mourning her passing, and I burst into hot, inexplicable tears.

There are no marks on her that I can see, but I remember that goshawk perched up in the big white gum tree at the back of the house. Perhaps it had a go at her and she had a heart attack; maybe it was waiting to collect her body when I went looking for her, and that's what the Mini-husbands were freaking out about. Free-range falconry.

She's not the only casualty of the red tooth and claw lately. The magpie geese have returned — ten this year. Helen has seen a juvenile limping near the edge of the top dam and says that although it can fly, it is obviously weak and distressed, so Geoffrey and I decide to catch it and see if it can be patched up, rather than leave it to that wretched feral cat.

We find it hiding in a patch of lantana; the leg is badly damaged. Somehow, the whole tendon to the foot has been severed. I bundle it up in the netting we used to catch it, and nurse it on my lap, while it tries to disappear by planting its head firmly under its wing.

Thank goodness the drive in the ute back to our place is only five minutes. The bugger is crawling with lice, and by now so am I, and Geoffrey is already undressed, hopping around with a can of insecticide, spraying his clothes, the floor and the front seat of the ute. The bird has got to go. The woman from the wildlife rescue service will know better than I what can be done for it. She's a volunteer, and drives all over the area as far north as Gladstone to rescue wild things. Her knowledge of wildlife is encyclopaedic and I am in awe of her dedication to her grand obsession.

I spend a lot of my time in awe. I have never been so completely awed in my entire life. Living has taken on a layer of intensity I never imagined. Everything I have experienced to this point is now magnified. Every taste, touch, every sensual perception has swelled, splitting my skin, leaking tears. Even my dreams are tear-sodden as my subconscious attempts to deal with this new open-pored way of living.

When the weather does get cold and the stars brighten in the clearer, cloudless skies of winter, we will set up our telescope to stare out into space and listen for the music of the spheres. I'll never forget seeing the mysterious rings of Saturn for the first time, sailing out there just as in the picture in my old primary-school *Jacaranda Atlas*. Why on earth it has taken me forty years to check it out for myself is the mystery. My mother has taken seventy years to jump at the opportunity, but she only wants to see the moon.

I tried to explain to her the feeling of seeing with eyes opened so wide that it will expand her vision way out beyond its normal depth of field. I don't think she gets what I mean, but I hope she will when she sees it — the realisation that no matter how far you extend your perception out from your physical boundary, the universe gets exponentially more elusive.

But I do my best to make sense of my small part of it, and feel utterly blessed to be living here with my love, under these stars in this particular paradise. We really are billion-year-old carbon, and I think we've made it — a couple of old hippies living in the world they imagined themselves into when they first had that sixteen-year-old crystal vision of what they would be when they grew up. At that age all I wanted to do was lie around with a gentle boy, play music, read and perhaps paint the odd picture. I don't remember the bit about digging out weeds or castrating baby bulls, but there's time here to fit them in.

In three short years this place has enveloped my consciousness. I've slid myself into it and pulled the flap down. When I remember the frenzy of the city, the distraction of that other glamorous reality, I realise that it is only possible to see the damage it can do from a distance. My body knew, though, even if the senses were deceived. My body was falling apart in its recoil from the state of over-excitement I was in — everything at boiling point, red-faced and angry. Not a good look, but you seldom get to see yourself from the outside, unless you are fortunate enough to have a coven of girlfriends who'll tell you, or a partner who is your perfect mirror, and both are as rare as hen's teeth.

Finally I'm at home, wearing *the shoes I'm in, the Earth I'm standing on*, and I now know what I'm hoping for. It wasn't clear at the start, merely a vague yearning for something just out of reach. I didn't know how to deal with the isolation, going from non-stop titillation to a dead stop. The body slowed down without any trouble — indeed, with a sigh of relief — but the mind went into a bit of a spin, till it found its focus. I'm pleased to say that Body and Mind have finally come to an arrangement and now happily keep each other honest.

Although Body would much rather hang out with the chooks and slog around in the garden, getting its hands dirty and a tan, Mind has put its foot down. The right time to sow fruiting annuals approaches, but till that day arrives, we won't go out into the beautiful day. Mind is having its way. No more lists of approach–avoidance tasks, no more diversionary tactics. Those times in my moon planting guide not dedicated to garden tasks are now dedicated to the studio. Body can just get used to getting its hands dirty *there*, tooling around in the fertile compost of Mind's new imaginary garden of delight.

It's nearly there. One more pale golden glaze to bind the whole surface with a uniform translucent veil, beneath which my lovely creamy eggs now glow, contrasted against a dark, shallow wooden bowl. And best of all, the original half-dozen has multiplied. I really *am* the mother of creation! During the process of making this one picture, new versions have materialised, and wait, like unfinished baby birds, to hatch into being, to leap out of the void into life.

I remember Mrs Mini's brooding patience and her capacity to overcome fear and hunger to stay on her nest. Still, quiet, withdrawn and completely inside herself for as long as it would take for the eggs to absorb all of her energy.

There. Finished.

I reach up and take a postcard down from the wall and hold it up beside my glistening new little painting. It is my yardstick of perfection. The postcard is only to jog the memory of having seen the real thing in all its staggering intensity at the National Gallery in London. To me it is the most beautiful thing in the world: *The Wilton Diptych*, a portable folding altarpiece from the twelfth century. On the left-hand side are four figures: the kneeling Richard II, his patron saint John the Baptist holding a lamb, and two others wearing opulent gowns. On the right is the most serene of Madonnas holding the Babe, surrounded by a quiver of angels, all robed in ethereal blue.

It is called *The Wilton Diptych* only because that is where it was found. The painter is anonymous — probably a monk whose body took its name with it to its grave, but the evidence of the life invested in that work is still vibrating, after all this time, with the energy of all the human hours it must have taken to make; all the love and devotion to stick at the task for long enough. When I stood in front of it, in the middle of the medieval galleries, the whole universe shrank to the space between my eyes and the surface of that mesmerising work of art.

There is, of course, no reasonable comparison between my modest little painting and the modest monk's, except that they are both painted in egg tempera. I will never reach his lofty place because it takes a whole lifetime to attain that level of skill. But at least now, having finished this one, I can see where I've been and how to proceed.

The time has come to turn the volume on the Minipecks down a notch.

I am completely sooky about murdering my Minis. I select the victim and pretend that I have no intent whatsoever — then *grab* … and try to minimise panicked flapping as much as possible. Once I have hold of it, we go for a bit of a stroll round the garden out of sight of the others and engage in a soothing conversation about world politics or global warming, till it calms down.

I feel its heart recover a regular beat, and gently lay it down on the block. There's no room for error. The stroke of my cane knife has to be sure and confident. An hour later, it sits gutted and trussed in my fridge, dinner for tomorrow night's anniversary feast.

It's not only the celebration of an event, but also acknowledgment of the sacrifice of this creature that has lost its life, and I'm going all out for this one. I've combed my recipe books for an appropriately exotic dish, and have all the ingredients I need. It'll be cooked in the new stove, and an excellent red is stashed away for the occasion.

Geoffrey is charged with composing grace.

And so it goes; the season turns. The sun will rise and set on another anniversary of the first day of the rest of the life we have left.

Geoffrey has come upstairs from his studio and put on the finished version of our new song. He joins me at the table to listen to us bound together by his music. As his verse rises towards my chorus, the voice in my head is already forming a harmony to its reassuring words:

In the end,
the beginning is the end
of another beginning …

As usual, my table groans under the muddle of my inner world. A single full-blown magenta rose stands in a slender, emerald-glazed vase, and a downy Minipeck feather rests lightly between the open pages of my garden diary. I'm working on this season's planting plans, sorting through seeds, and making notes, as Evan watches over my thoughts from his image on the wall above. This year there are new additions to the clutter: a sketchbook and a varnished wooden case containing all my drawing materials sit beside the red toolbox.

Acknowledgments

I respectfully acknowledge the Gubbi Gubbi people, traditional owners of *the earth I'm standing on*.

Eternal gratitude and love to Rose Creswell for admitting me to the highest order of pleasure in a literary life, to Geoffrey Datson for everything, including the use of his poetry, and to our families for their support. Grateful thanks to the extraordinary Judith Lukin-Amundsen and Mary Rennie for their editorial genius, and to the entire HarperCollins team for, well, everything else. And thanks to the coven for your loyalty, best-girlfriendship, and being pleased for me to name my chooks after you.

The verses I quote from the Bible are Genesis 3:6 and Isaiah 9:6. Apart from the snatches of Milton from *Paradise Lost* (Book IX), the epigraph from Raina Maria Rilke's *Letters to a Young Poet*, and 'Man that is Born of Woman', which is from the Book of Common Prayer, all the poetry and songs quoted in the book are by Geoffrey Datson. 'Ketaminefield', which I quote from selectively, follows these acknowledgments in full.

Other titles mentioned are Linda Woodrow's *The Permaculture Home Garden* (Penguin, Melbourne, 1996), Katie Thear and Alistair Fraser's *The Complete Book of Raising Livestock and Poultry* (Pan, London, 1968). The Margaret Olley biography is by Meg Stewart, *Far from a Still Life* (Random House, Sydney, 2005).

My blog is at www.hughesy.journalspace.com, where I have posted images of the paintings and audio of the songs discussed in the book, as well as related links. Our music can be found at www.stickylabel.com.au

Ketaminefield

Beneath the gilded domes
flaked leaf paper altar burn.
Collapse inwards,
your garden of Eden unfolds
within the eye of God.

Pantheon of clouds stream o'erhead
past iris, tulip, pupil.
Bulb of all knowledge,
flickers in a half light so intense,
of ten million light years.

You who have read to me
memories of mother,
laid upon mother,
laid upon mother
back into the earth.

The fragile grid
of all our race histories
held tender to heart
and wrapped as heirlooms,
silent under care.

So soft
as not a hare's breath
disturbs
utter, rapt
concentration.

Prayers,
passed forward
mother to son,
son to daughter,
daughter to child,

And you said:
'Look only
at six paintings,
because the seventh
is you.'

This Easter,
symmetrical but not quite,
in smell so sacred
we know it
in the dark night of the soul.

Across a crowded dance floor,
shimmer, the fabric of time,
slow spinning,
magnetic in gyroscope
transparent globe, flux, field.

Forever is never through
the portal of consciousness,
as true poet
is fenestration
of the fire word.

Geoffrey Datson, 2004